The Time Traveler

The Time Traveler

Ivan Pereira Mendonça

Mendonca, Ivan Pereira de
     The time traveler / Ivan
Pereira de Mendonca ; [tradução do autor].
-- Macaé, RJ : Ed. do Autor, 2024.
Título original: O viajante do tempo.
ISBN 978-65-01-39209-7
1. Ficção brasileira I. Título.
25-260894 CDD-B869.3
Índices para catálogo sistemático:
1. Ficção : Literatura brasileira
B869.3
Eliane de Freitas Leite - Bibliotecária - CRB 8/8415

Time traveler refers to the

6th Chakra – Light – Pineal gland – connection with spirituality/intuition

Responsible for inner PEACE / inner/outer alignment

Blocked by illusion

ICAR (Roman Catholic Apostolic Church) – Pride

Arrogance in not recognizing reality – we are all prisoners/criminals

John the Baptist – writes the church of Philadelphia – reward "to become the pillar of the temple"

The Ajna chakra is the chakra of the will that is <u>subjugated</u> when one assumes the submissive position of the Catholic Jesus.

Time traveler highlights the imprisonment of consciousness

– Sansara – where the character is trapped in his own perception of problems through several lives until he is finally freed by his own conscience

P reface
	Visitors to ancient ruins often report an overwhelming experience when they come face to face with these ancient symbols, and a sense of profound loss as they contemplate the mysterious inscriptions on the ancient monuments. The question arises: what have we left behind? Who were these hybrid deities, depicted as part-human beings? And who were these extraordinary figures of size, depicted with an air of grandeur? It seems that knowledge of what these texts and images meant has been forgotten over time.

The lack of information about these civilizations and their innovations leads many to believe that advanced technology existed in ancient times, including methods of forging metals, forms of clean energy, and feats of civil engineering that still defy modern understanding.

The sages foresaw this oblivion when they stated that, one day, the inscriptions written on monoliths and temple walls would be all that would remain of the vast knowledge, in fact, the records remained unknown, unintelligible to the generations that came after.

How does the knowledge of entire civilizations come to an end? In 30 BC, the death of Cleopatra, the last pharaoh of Egypt, marked the end of dynastic Egypt, which was incorporated into the Roman Empire. Centuries later, in 381 AD, Emperor Theodosius, in an effort to unify the beliefs of all his subjects, banned all pagan religions, ending ancestral cults, mythologies and esoteric sects.

This cultural erasure during invasions and colonizations has been a recurring strategy in history, where the imposition of control occurs not only over the territory, but also over cultural memory.

This process was not restricted to a single place or to a single ancient memory. In South America, for example, when the European conquerors arrived in the 15th century, there was a deliberate extinction of sacred traditions and texts and many indigenous priests were persecuted. As for the MU continent, the few records found are considered to be fictional tales (James-Churchward - The Lost Continent of MU). Thus, many cultural narratives were lost, and the history of these civilizations ended up fragmented or rewritten under new domains.

As the centuries passed and under different rulers or through the imposition of new religions and beliefs, the human race's knowledge of the past was fading away.

So, I decided to write this book to record all the experience that I ended up living in my introspections and meditations, this is a practice that I acquired as a result of having studied Rosicrucianism and other mystery schools, I ended up going deep into my own mind and exploring various aspects that many people believe do not exist.

All the techniques mentioned in this book are not fiction, but rather a reality experienced by me and which I believe can be practiced by the reader as long as he is not afraid to penetrate his own consciousness. For this, no special tool or device will be necessary, just patience and tranquility.

The places mentioned throughout the story, although presented superficially, are real and carry profound historical meanings. Among them are Ollantaytambo, an ancient Inca site in the

Sacred Valley of Peru; Tiahuanaco, a mysterious archaeological center in Bolivian lands that holds the secrets of an ancient civilization; and Al Naslaa, a fascinating rock formation in the Tayma oasis in Saudi Arabia, known for its incredible natural fissure. Villages that were just beginning to flourish at the time the story takes place are also mentioned, such as Harappa and Moenjodaro, located in the Indus River Valley in the region of India, the birthplace of one of the first and most advanced urban civilizations of antiquity. It is important to remember, however, that the story presented here is entirely based on fiction. Any similarity to real events is purely coincidental, as the purpose of the text is to illustrate the flow of incarnations through the ages, exploring the wheel of samsara, as described in the traditions of Hinduism.

The narrative of this book evokes images of imposing cities, formed by monumental skyscrapers that, ironically, only now, in 2024, are beginning to be built in reality, as is the case with the visionary megaprojects of Saudi Arabia. The inspiration for this futuristic vision, however, comes not from the desert landscapes of the Middle East, but rather from the majestic natural formations of Chapada Diamantina, in northern Brazil.

It is the vastness of the plateaus and the imposing rocky walls that shaped these fictional cities, where the grandeur of nature blends with human ingenuity in a bold architecture. This mixture of influences transforms the Brazilian landscape into a starting point for imagining a past (or future) in which nature and technology coexisted in perfect harmony.

Walter Russel, in "A New Concept of the Universe" and James Churchward in "The Lost Continent of Mu" are two books that present theories and facts about the distant past that may be of interest to the seeker. I mention them here as a reading recommendation because they are already "old" writings and easily obtained on the international network without any harm to the authors.

The beginning of everything

Normally people don't even think about the place where their own memories are stored, not those on the computer or the phone, but our own memories. If we ask any doctor, psychologist or scholar of the mind, they will tell you that it is somewhere in the brain. But I have my doubts about this. Some scholars of the spirit claim that memories are stored throughout the body, which is partly true, but everything we experience is somehow recorded in time itself in the so-called akashic records.

I really don't know how to explain it, but after a lot of effort I managed to partially unlock all my memories. In fact, I embarked on a process of self-knowledge and my goal was to understand the world we live in, as I had gone through an experience that had left a deep impression on me. In order for it to be recorded and accessible to you, who are now reading this book, the best way I know is through writing, because even after I have passed through this life, my writings will be available, as long as these records exist, so that anyone can read and believe or not what I say.

I didn't bother to look for evidence about the things I experienced, for a very simple reason, I simply experienced them and remembered them, in the same way that you can, with little effort, remember some important date in your life, for example the day your child was born, or some banal accident that was recorded in your memory. You can remember that fact from your life without needing to see a photograph, which would be proof, but even without this proof, it is there in your memory because it happened to you, and under normal conditions you can't deny that it didn't happen. This was my case, the things I remembered, for me, were past events. Of course, in some cases I researched and found more information in order to verify the story, but this was only in some cases because I didn't really feel the need to do so.

I believe that anyone who follows the same path will obtain similar results and will then be able to analyze whether what I write is my daydreaming or stories I have experienced.

<hr>

Osho was once asked, "Is there life after death?" To which he replied, "That is a wrong, meaningless question. One should never jump ahead of oneself; there is every chance that one will fall flat on one's face."

You have to ask the basic question, start from the beginning. My suggestion is to ask a more basic question.

For example, you might ask:

"Is there life after birth?

"That would be more basic, because many people are born, but few have life.

Just being born is not enough for you to have life. You exist, certainly, but life is more than mere existence. You were born, but unless you are reborn into your being, you do not live, you never live.

Osho, in "The Book of Living and Dying"

I think this was the case with Sandra, my girlfriend. I met Sandra in 1990. I was 17 and she was 16. That's when I returned to Rio de Janeiro. Before that, I lived in Macaé. I was born in Niterói, the former capital of the state of Rio de Janeiro. Then my parents had to move to Macaé/RJ because my father owned a company that provided services to oil exploration companies and I had to go with them. After all, I was 14 and a dependent. Then I came to the capital to study and take my naval engineering course, and I ended up meeting her. Sandra was different, she didn't even seem like a girl who lives in a big city, her short life had been spent only studying and going to church, she didn't even know the city where she lived completely, the famous places in Rio de Janeiro she visited with me, together we went to Sugarloaf Mountain, Corcovado, but our favorite place was Parque Burle, a large garden, we spent hours walking around that wonderful place, unfortunately her life ended prematurely, after being killed in a robbery at a bus stop in the neighborhood where we lived.

My name is Paulo, I work in a bank, I started as an intern at the bank as soon as I came to live in Rio de Janeiro, I studied at night and worked at the bank as an office boy, it was a bit of a busy life but I was very satisfied with everything I was doing until the incident with Sandra happened.

I had arranged to meet her at a bus stop, a place we always used because we lived nearby and it was a routine route for us, but that Saturday afternoon we still had to decide where to go. I was already a little late when I saw her a short distance away, about twenty or thirty meters if I'm not mistaken, being mugged and reacting to the kid who was pulling her bag. In a fraction of a second I saw him fire the fateful shot, he fired and ran down the street amidst the cars that were passing by. All I could do was hug her in her last moments because she had fallen and I couldn't do anything else that was worthwhile. I only had the opportunity to stay there, hug her and witness the tragedy. She didn't say anything, she couldn't because of the fright and the shot that had hit her heart.

At that moment I didn't know that another change in my life was happening, but that accident that destroyed Sandra's life and all of our plans, was more than just shocking to me, it was an event that made all the difference in my life, to this day I don't know how I managed to tell her parents, it was such a big upset that it caused me that I spent a few days without really understanding what had happened, and with that scene repeating itself in my memory, I was out of my senses, so to speak, and that was what really led me on a search that for me in those days would be beyond imagination.

After the initial sadness and all the problems that sudden loss causes, I felt a sense of loss and at the same time a sense of helplessness that I couldn't overcome. So, like everyone else, I looked for something that would comfort me. I didn't try any illicit drugs, religion or spiritualism, because I have many doubts about that. Although the appeal of Marcos, her cousin and our mutual friend, and her parents, who attend church, was quite strong and insistent, I couldn't explain it in those days, but religion was simply something that didn't have much meaning for me. I knew the main points of some religions, because I had already read about some, but nothing made me believe in a "persona" god who is in heaven "judging" the living and the dead, as the Catholic religion teaches, nor the need for faith in the impossible, as some others preach.

One day, we met on the street and he invited me for a coffee, I think our friendship ended that day due to an opinion we expressed to each other and he ended up considering me a being possessed by the devil or something worse, at some point he said to me,

– God took her because He knows what is best for her. He said this referring to Sandra because it had been a few months since she passed to the other side of life.

So I answered him without thinking:

– If He knows and keeps it to Himself, we have no way of knowing whether this God is good or bad.

– You can't judge God, that's how He wants it. Marcos replied.

– That's exactly why I think this whole religion thing is just a soft conversation for cattle to snore, you say that's how He wants it and that's it, end of conversation, the search for a real reason ends here with this conversation, we are forced to conform and that's it.

-- I simply don't believe in this God that you believe in, for me this is just a figment of people's imagination, he is as real as Thor or Odin.

-- Man, look at how perfect nature is, look at the greatness of the universe, how can you not believe in God? He told me

-- The fact that there is an organized nature and a vast universe does not mean that there is a mind with human characteristics behind it. I replied

-- But the Bible says that we are made in his image and likeness.

-- Bible, whoever wrote it would say that this God is like, similar to what? What other form of consciousness would he have as a basis to report besides our image, imagine if whoever wrote it would put there that God is similar to a supercomputer and has the shape of a Pen drive, he said that and I saw Marcos change color.

-- I'm afraid of you with these statements of yours, said Marcos.

-- Why ?

-- Because an unbelieving person like you always brings bad luck to you and those close to you, and they end up being manipulated by the facts they attract.

-- What do you mean? You mean that because I don't have this imaginary friend, bad things can happen to me and my friends?

-- That's right, your mental attitude attracts evil into your life, science is beginning to discover these things, in fact this is a demonic influence that is acting on you, making you an unbeliever and doubting the word of God, in other words, you are being manipulated by the forces of evil.

-- For me, when you watch a movie where the main character is a criminal and you end up rooting for the criminal to succeed in the story, then you are being manipulated, or when you are led to believe that you are defending the cause of a minority, putting ethics in second place, that is manipulation.

-- A film is just a film, it doesn't influence my life, and who or what would be behind this manipulation, and for what purpose?

-- I don't know, but for me this is very clear, it is a distortion of ethics, of the normal meaning of things, I learned that a criminal is a criminal, and that a good criminal is a dead criminal, that ethics as well as the equality of people must always be a priority.

--It's not always like this, each case is different, you are being radical, and I'm just going to tell you one thing; Soon things will happen in your life and you will see how wrong you are, for now I'm going to pray that you will be relieved of this burden of disbelief and that you will begin to see that superior forces govern our lives and that God will enlighten you and the light of truth will shine in your life.

Marcos said these things and left apparently indignant, he forgot to pay for the coffee, it was on me, thank goodness it was just one coffee.

I stood there for a few moments at the counter of the cafeteria thinking about that encounter, because for me the force behind everything is financial power, governments and everything else I know, exist according to the world's driving force, money, and there are no superior or inferior forces to interfere in the lives of others, there are people with imaginations willing to distort the truth of the facts, people terrified by the fear instilled in the back of their minds and capable of atrocities beyond imagination, often in the name of some religion, or to promote good in an apparently philanthropic way, everything under the sun is false. If it could have some meaning that had gone unnoticed, after all, without thinking, I had opened a box in my mind and from it some demons that were kept there could come out, and I didn't give them any importance, but perhaps it would be worth examining in more depth sometime, I paid for the coffee and went back to work.

At the end of the day, those words from Marcos still reverberated in my mind: "Soon things will happen in your life and you will see how wrong you are." Although I didn't believe he was some kind of psychic with the ability to predict the future, I was impressed and thought about it for the rest of the day as if it were a warning.

It was a summer day and I was riding my newly purchased motorcycle along Copacabana beach after work when, stopped at a traffic light, a boy handed me a piece of advertising about past life therapy, "understand your future by knowing what your past was like". Of course I thought it was a cheap scam to fool suckers, but I ended up keeping the paper, I couldn't throw it on the street and when I got home, when I emptied my pockets I came across the ad again, I don't know why I put it on the table without paying much attention to what was written.

Until one day after work, I stopped by Mr. José's newsstand, which was on the corner near my house, and bought a newspaper so I could read something different. After reading the entire newspaper, and having nothing else to read, I went to read the classifieds, the part where you can find ads for meetings, religious people, and masseurs, and I found the ad again that said, "Past life regression."

I wouldn't have thought about looking for regression if it weren't for a dream I had the night before. It was a strange dream, one of those that seems real and that really impressed me. I dreamed that I was on top of a pyramid. There were several trees where it was located, which made me rule out it being an Egyptian pyramid, a pyramid in the middle of the forest, perhaps in Central America. But it was very large and smooth, it seemed mirrored. After that scene, I found myself in a meeting with several very strange people, dressed in clothes made of metal and fabric. Best of all, I was a kind of boss of those people. Everyone looked at me and gave me some kind of greeting before leaving, as if they were paying homage. I also noticed the presence of a very beautiful woman, and I felt a lot of love for her. She came to talk to me, held out her hand to me, and I woke up, wanting to know more about that scene. I certainly hadn't dreamed about Sandra, but it was something that really intrigued me. Who were those people, that place, and who was the woman? I had never seen a scene like that in a movie or in a book. How can we dream about what we don't know, that was a rare moment of joy, because after Sandra's death I was in a complicated situation, I went to work, to college, came back, but boredom was taking over me, I felt like I was losing my taste for everything and that moment was important because it gave me the feeling that life hadn't stopped and that I still had a lot to achieve, so I decided that I would somehow satisfy my curiosity.

It was on a Monday morning, when I arrived at work, carrying my helmet, that Dona Sueli came to talk to me.

-- Now you come to work by motorcycle?

-- Yes, I couldn't take the bus anymore, my parents wanted me to have a car, but I preferred a motorbike because it's much faster in traffic, and parking here in the center is much easier.

-- So is the bike yours? Do you have insurance?

-- I haven't thought about it yet. Sueli was the bank's insurance manager, an acquaintance of my father, as were the other bank managers, and of course, she was offering me motorcycle insurance.

-- For employees there is a special discount, payroll deduction, do it now, just bring me a copy of her documents and I will resolve it for you today.

--Wait a minute, I'll do it, I replied. I quickly made copies of the documents she asked for and gave them to her that morning.

-- Great, the insurance coverage will be valid from tomorrow.

-- But is it that fast? I asked

-- Normally not, but in your case I'll find a way to do it as quickly as possible.

I thought that was a strange attitude, as if she knew something was going to happen, but I preferred not to bring up the subject right away.

The next day, at the end of the workday, I looked for Sueli and asked her about the special treatment with the motorcycle insurance.

-- I found it strange, but tell me why my motorcycle insurance came out so quickly?

-- Actually, I brought the process forward and asked the bank's headquarters to do it faster. They responded to me.

--And what was the special reason?

-- It was nothing major, I just dreamed that you came in here with a helmet in your hand and I sold you motorcycle insurance.

--Of course it wasn't just that, did you dream that I fell and broke everything or that my motorcycle was stolen?

-- Not at all, it wasn't like that at all, I just dreamed about the scene, in my dream you were at the bank and asked me about insurance, like any other customer.

-- It doesn't justify you doing it faster than normal, of course there was more that you don't want to tell

-- It wasn't just that, it was Alberto, my husband, who after I told him about the dream, he told me to do it as quickly as I could because you might need it, I didn't even know you had a motorcycle.

-- Is he serious about this dream business?

-- He teaches Yoga, practices meditation, does a few other things and yes, he takes these subjects related to psychology, dreams, the unconscious very seriously, that's his thing.

-- Wow, that's right, I'd like to talk to him, because I've already had a dream that seemed very real to me and it's recurring, it's happened three times.

-- Come to my house on Saturday, you can talk to him and maybe he will teach you some practice that you like.

So on Saturday morning I went to her house, it was an old house on Rua dos Oitis, a very tree-lined and quiet street in Gávea, I rang the doorbell and Alberto answered right away, who I didn't know yet, but he was a tall guy, with white hair and skin and a unkempt beard, apparently a little older than Sueli, who appeared shortly after.

-- Good morning Paulo,

-- Good morning Sueli. Alberto saw that we knew each other and took a step back, without saying anything.

-- Come in, Alberto, this is Paulo, from the bank who I told you about.

-- Yes, there is, the motorcycle one, and did you get insurance? Alberto asked me, now more relaxed.

-- Yes, we did, Sueli scared me, she said she dreamed that I fell off the motorcycle and suffered a loss, so I got the insurance as soon as possible. I took a risk.

-- Well, she didn't tell me that part about you falling, she told me something else.

The house had a side hallway and a door that led to a living room. This was where Alberto had a kind of studio and, in addition to other activities, he taught Yoga classes. In the living room near the entrance, there was a small table and two armchairs, one on each side of a sofa. The rest was the space where, it seemed to me, people practiced during classes, as it was quite large. There must have been room for about twenty people with their mats spread out. So we sat down there.

-- Dreams are actually the subconscious showing its concerns, so we should take this very seriously. You mentioned a fall, was that your invention or a dream? Alberto told me.

-- It was my invention, I was intrigued because Sueli got me the insurance very quickly and I thought there was some reason and she hadn't said it

-- There was no other reason, I just recommended that she get the insurance as soon as possible because she had dreamed that you were looking for her to get the insurance, so I thought it would be a risk for you, but that was it, her dream ended, but she told me that you are having a recurring dream, tell me about it.

-- That's right, Alberto, I dreamed that I was in a pyramid, outside of it, there was a forest around this pyramid, it was smooth and shiny, then I climbed up a kind of floating platform that went to the top of the pyramid.

-- Then I found myself in a meeting with some people who were supposed to be the bosses of that place, and everyone greeted me and left, then a tall, dark-haired woman appeared and extended her hand to me so we could leave too, then I woke up, but I have the feeling that that woman is someone I know, that gives me a disturbing feeling because I can't remember who it could be, then Sueli told me that you study these subjects and I came here looking for some guidance.

-- Disturbing feeling, can you explain to me better what you mean by that? Alberto asked me

-- Well, at the beginning of last year I lost my girlfriend, but the woman in the dream has nothing to do with her. In reality I feel something that I can't quite explain, I miss her, it's like a longing, but I think it's more like nostalgia, can you understand me?

-- He looked at me deeply as if he saw something through me, he stood still for almost a minute with that expressionless look that was making me embarrassed, suddenly he asked me.

-- What do you believe in?

-- What do you mean? In what sense?

-- Religion, God, angels, demons, heaven, hell, what do you believe in?

-- I don't believe in religion, I was raised in a Kardecist spiritualist family, but I also don't believe in the things they say there, I think it's all very fanciful, healing passes, obsessive spirits, for me it's all imagination.

-- And do you believe in past lives?

-- Not me either! I replied, not understanding where he was going with that.

-- So what do you think happens when a person dies?

-- I haven't died yet, so I've never thought about it, but I think it all ends. I've even been thinking about looking for someone who does past life consultations because I saw an ad that talked about it, but I don't know.

-- There are people doing therapy, they say it's past life regression and they do a hypnosis session, something I don't approve of. I'm starting a practice, it's experimental, do you want to participate with me?

--I've heard of regression and I'm interested, but I don't think you'll be able to hypnotize me into doing it. I replied.

-- And who said anything about hypnosis? This method is different, I don't do hypnosis because there are people who are not sincere and this ends up causing problems, there are many cases of people being deceived by hypnotists who take advantage of those being hypnotized, so I don't even do that.

-- Well, in that case I accept, so what do you do?

-- I give some meditation practices to my yoga students. In meditation, we have several forms. There is contemplative meditation, in which the person meditates by concentrating on an image or something similar, like a saint for example. There is meditation on emptiness. There is psychological meditation, which is what I explore. Believe me, there are people who can meditate while they are doing some repetitive activity.

Sueli explained to me that some therapists use mental regression (DVT) to discover the causes of chronic problems in their patients, such as phobias, headaches without a specific cause, aversions to hospitals and certain common situations, but that this was not his case, as it was an experiment he was carrying out for his psychology studies, and I would be a guinea pig, but there would be no danger whatsoever.

-- I can meditate while I'm sweeping the house. Sueli added after getting into the subject.

-- I've seen people meditating while listening to hymns of praise. I completed.

-- Yes, but we cannot always call it meditation. True meditation alters the electrical states of the brain. Science recognizes four vibrational states: Beta, the common waking state; Alpha, when the frequency decreases and breathing slows down; Theta, where electrical impulses decrease even more and deep meditation occurs; and the Delta state, which is the deepest state yet. I work by inducing these last two states, but I will warn you, not just anyone can do it.

-- Geez, but how will I know if I can do it? I asked naively.

-- Well, the quickest way is to practice, but you need to have courage and the will to enter your mind, the one who enters is you, no one else, during hypnosis the hypnotist is the one who comes into contact with your mind, that's why it's dangerous.

-- Cool, I want to do it, how much do you charge?

-- As I said, it's experimental, so I don't charge, I just need you to commit, because I prepare myself to do it, I set aside time, so it really just depends on you.

-- That's all right, so what will it be like then?

-- Can you come every Saturday afternoon? Is that a good time for you?

-- Yes, but have you ever done this with someone else?

-- I've already done it, you'll be the fifth person I've done it with, the first one gave up, he was afraid of what he might see, the second one had no commitment, so I was the one who gave up and with the other two it worked out quite well, one is already finished and we're still doing the other one.

-- So I won't do it alone?

-- No, but that's an individual thing, we'll do it at different times.

Deal done, we went for a coffee and then I left that Saturday and something told me that memory regression therapy would serve as research, perhaps a self-analysis, although I knew almost nothing of what awaited me, I confess that I learned to trust my feelings and rare intuitions.

Monday started with a light and persistent rain that would stay there until Thursday or Friday to further discolor my anguish, everything happened slowly and leisurely until on Saturday I was there again, me and Alberto.

On the wall of the studio there were shelves with many books, some of which I already knew, Alberto positioned the armchair better and asked me to sit there.

-- It is reclining, lie down well because you will need to relax

-- I'm going to end up sleeping here. I said as I reclined the backrest.

-- No, you won't, I need to explain a few things to you. A lot of what I study and practice comes from Hinduism, from the Vedas, which is a very ancient wisdom. According to this, our subtle body has five layers that are called Koshas, which means sheaths. I understand by layers, the densest layer is the physical body, the vital energy body, which can even be seen with some training, the instinctive and intellectual body, the cognitive mental body and the blissful body, that is, the divine body.

So when we die, or rather when the body dies, the other bodies remain and the memory with them, when the soul reincarnates, the brain has nothing, it is clean, without impressions and memories, then the ego is formed and does not allow those memories to be reviewed, that is why very rarely does someone remember a past life, but a good part of it is there and we access it through a very deep meditation.

-- Does Hinduism teach this? I asked curiously.

-- No, it doesn't teach, I mean, it teaches in part, but a lot of it is my theory.

-- In Hinduism, in the Vedas, there are three gods, which are Brahma, Vishnu and Shiva, who are the representation of forms of consciousness, with Shiva being the expression of the consciousness of all living beings, Brahma the expression of the consciousness of all space and Vishnu the expression of the consciousness of all matter, of course no Brahmin will explain it to you in this way, this is my understanding and my way of explaining.

-- Brahmin? What is this?

-- They are the priests, so to speak, of Hinduism, the masters and owners of Vedic knowledge.

-- So for you to meditate, it will be easier if you concentrate on God Brahma, and empty your thoughts, you don't need an image for that, do you?

-- I don't think so. I replied.

I was getting interested in what he had to say about Hinduism. I had already read something about the Vedas, but very superficially, and about other religions too. I had already read a good part of the Quran of Islam. I had already read the Bible of Judaism, and in the end I ended up thinking that everything that is said about religions is just fantasies that have been transformed over time. But I found his interpretation very personal and I didn't think I should criticize it at that moment. After all, discussing religion was not my goal.

-- So look at that painting on the wall in front of you. Alberto said this, stood up, turned off the lights in the room and turned on a lamp pointing at a painting that I had already seen but hadn't paid attention to yet.

It was a large painting measuring about 2x2 meters, all in black and white, with an image in the center made with horizontal lines about 2cm wide, each line changing color, sometimes black, sometimes white, forming the image of Ying and Yang. There were no borders or frames, just the lines forming the image and nothing else.

-- Can we start? Alberto asked.

-- Yes, I'm listening to you.

-- First you need to relax, can you do it? Or would you prefer me to guide you?

-- I'd rather you guide me, I'm a little agitated today.

-- Start by relaxing your feet..., he waited a moment, and continued. Relaxing your legs..., he waited another moment, and continued. Relaxing your hands..., relaxing your arms...

Soon I felt that something wasn't going as it should, a tingling sensation in my face started to take away my concentration and I simply couldn't relax, and I started to move around in that reclining chair.

-- Paulo, you can't relax, can you?

-- Yes, I'm not, it feels like there's something bothering me and I don't know what it is.

-- Don't worry, it's hard to get it the first time.

-- So what are we going to do? I asked disappointedly.

-- Well, this is the way, it's just a matter of preparation, practice this relaxation during the week and next week we'll do it again.

-- What do you mean, train?

-- That's right, practice relaxation, do it in parts, mentally switch off parts of your body until only your thoughts remain, forget about the TV for a while and try to have a calmer mind.

-- But I'll end up falling asleep.

-- There is no problem if you sleep, but when you wake up, don't get up quickly. When you wake up, mentally return to relaxation and do it slowly, without rushing to move. Feel your body relaxed and gradually become aware of it. Do this whenever you can and next week we will have a different result. Another thing, you can practice this disconnection during the day as well, at any interval you can practice it. Do it every day. Condition your mind to this.

I thought about starting to practice that Saturday, but as soon as I got home a friend invited me to go to the city of Itaipava/RJ, a short motorcycle trip, about 200 km round trip. Since I had never been on a motorcycle trip, I accepted right away. I learned to ride a motorcycle in Macaé, then I bought my motorcycle in Niterói, which is about twenty kilometers from home. The only trip I took was across the bridge that connects the two cities, with lots of cars, so it was an opportunity to see several things that I couldn't pass up.

The following day, a very cloudy Sunday, promising rain, I prepared a backpack with waterproof clothing as it could rain and we set off on the two bikes, Maurício in front as he knew the way and I followed him a short distance behind.

At the exit of the city there is a toll booth, right after it is the climb of the mountain with the most beautiful landscape I had ever seen and it only ends very close to the city of Petrópolis, halfway we stopped at a place called the Mirante do Cristo from where you can see a statue of a crucified Jesus facing the city of Rio de Janeiro which is at the bottom of the valley, I think it is an aberration this idea of putting an image of a cross with a person nailed to it, in full torture, but it is the tradition of Catholics I think, we continued on.

Arriving in the small town of Itaipava we stopped at a small shopping mall to have lunch and rest a little from the trip, it was already very sunny and there was no chance of rain like there was when we left home.

--You didn't tell me what you came to do here in this place. I asked Maurício with the intention of starting a conversation.

--I didn't come to do anything! He answered me, a little embarrassed.

--What do you mean, do nothing?

--I like to go out and rest my mind, that's all. Sometimes I wander around the city aimlessly, but the traffic isn't good, so when time allows, I prefer to go on the road. Whenever I can, I go to a neighboring city, then return refreshed. I thought you might like to go up the mountains.

--Yes, I really liked it, the climb is very beautiful. I already knew it but I had never climbed it on a motorcycle, it was my first time traveling by motorcycle, but I wouldn't do it with the intention of resting, I prefer to stay at home and read a book.

--But you live alone, don't you?

--Yes, I live here on the river.

--Well, I live with four other people, because of that there is never peace at home, when I have to study I go to the library because at home I simply can't. I have a younger sister and a younger brother, they are always fighting, my sister plays volleyball on the beach, she is very competitive, my brother is a rocker and jealous, they are always at war.

--If you need a quiet place, you can count on my apartment, it's very quiet there, during the week I don't go there, I'm almost never at home, but on the weekends I'm always at home.

--And do you have a girlfriend?

--She died, almost a year ago.

--What do you mean, she found someone else and didn't want anything to do with you anymore, or did you just leave her?

--He died reacting to a robbery, he was shot and did not resist

--Wow, sorry for the joke, I didn't imagine that kind of thing.

--It's okay, life goes on.

We stayed there talking about motorcycles and riding for over an hour, then we returned. The descent from the mountain is on another track, not as beautiful as the ascent, but still a worthwhile trip. On the way back, I noticed how the brain adapts to different situations in which we end up putting ourselves in. For example, when I ride the motorcycle in traffic, I am always concerned about the movement of other vehicles around me, but on the road, my attention is very different. I pay more attention to the speed I am going and to any upcoming curves, much less attention to any obstacles that might get in the way. Because of this, it becomes more comfortable for the mind, depending on the speed, it is almost like meditation.

I was thinking about the reasons for the trip that Maurício claimed, to get away from his family to have peace, to find peace on the road at 120 km per hour, I wonder if he would be able to achieve a deep relaxation like the one I am aiming to practice.

It was starting to get dark when we passed the toll booth that greets us at the entrance to the city, which caused us some apprehension due to the violence that exists in that region, so without exchanging a word we kept the pace we were going until we got home. Maurício went to Tijuca, the neighborhood where he lives, we would only meet on Monday at the college.

Once home, I remembered the practice that Alberto told me to do to prepare myself for the next section, after doing my home routine, after all the next day would be a Monday which is normally busy, I sat on the floor, at the foot of the bed, leaned back and started to relax my mind, I remembered the road, the curves and that our brain always looks for the most comfortable situation to feel better, I relaxed.

I don't think I actually slept there on the floor, cross-legged, leaning against a cushion. It was early when I sat down, it must have been about twenty or twenty-thirty. At some point I found myself back in the room with the people in their strange clothes, and the woman, who I decided to call the red woman because of her skin, looked like an Indian, except she was tall and thin, with straight hair, and of an especially remarkable beauty. Then she came closer to me, in fact she came very close, as if she were going to kiss me. She looked straight into my eyes, put her hands on my face and said something. I didn't understand her words, but I knew immediately what they meant: "Don't forget to come back to me."

After that, my consciousness began to return to its normal state, a huge numbness in my body, I thought it was because of the fatigue from the trip, prevented me from making any movement for a few minutes, but then I got up and saw that it was two o'clock, I had literally been out for five hours that seemed like only a few minutes. After that, I decided that I would do anything to find out who the red woman was.

I continued practicing relaxation every day until the next Saturday. Until then, I hadn't realized how much we are connected to mental activity without rest. Then we have problems sleeping at night, always watching something on TV or, at best, reading a book, but never resting our thoughts and stopping our mind from working. I had never done that.

On Saturday afternoon, there I was with Alberto again to start the experience; I had practiced meditation and relaxation all week and most of the time I was successful, now it was the final test.

-- Lie down and relax your body as much as possible, but don't fall asleep. He said as he darkened the room, leaving only a light directed at the psychedelic painting in front of me.

_Don't worry, I won't sleep.

He began to speak, asking me to relax my body, initially through my feet, then my legs, until finally closing my eyes, then I felt in a state of torpor, a waking sleeper and strangely I answered his questions without difficulty.

_ Where do you live,

_Palm Trees Street, Botafogo

--Imagine yourself there, and describe to me what you see on that street.

_ Yes, I'm at home, I see the stove, the refrigerator, the sofa bed, the television, the open window...

-- Go to the window describe to me--what you see

-- I see the waning moon, the old supermarket building, the old houses on the other street that are backed by the building, the buildings on the other street...

-- Now I want you to remember when you were 12 years old.

-- Yes, what do you want to know?

-- Tell me what comes to your mind first.

-- Marina, my schoolmate, we studied in the same class for a few years, we are friends

-- Let's fast forward a little further, tell me about when you were 15 years old.

--I don't study at Salesiano anymore, I'm going to Macaé, with my parents, we're going to live there

--Do you remember the house you went to live in?

--Yes, a very comfortable house, close to the beach, I remember what my room was like.

--Go to the door, but don't open it, stop in front of the door.

--Yes, I'm in front of the door.

-- When you open this door, you will enter a tunnel, I will count to 10 while you go through this tunnel and when you come out at the end of it you will be in a past life, a life before this one. He said this and began counting, very slowly, and I went through that imaginary tunnel, at the end, suddenly I found myself in another place, another scene.

I saw myself lying down in the shade of a tree, a huge olive tree.

_ Where are you now? Alberto asked me.

--Coimbra Council, harvesting olives. It took me a while to understand that it was about olives, in that vision I was very young and already working in the harvest on the farm where I lived, but what was really strange was that the words came out of my mouth

without me thinking about the answer, it seemed like it was someone else answering.

-- Do you know the year in which you are harvesting olives?

-- It is the year of our Lord 1852

-- And how old is the harvester?

-- 15 years

_Tell me what it was like when you were 8 years old, in this life
that is in your memory.

_ I'm at home, I help my mother, it's just one room, we live on
a farm, we work here.

_Can you tell me in general terms, that is, in a few words, the
important facts of this life?

_ Until I was sixteen I stayed on the farm, then I went to the
city to work in the factory, I'm a loader. . .

--I want you to go into the tunnel and fast forward to when the
harvester is 20 years old.

I entered the tunnel again and walked a few steps, I found myself in another place.

--I'm in the city, I work in a small warehouse, it's a weaving
mill, I'm a helper

--You have someone with you, friend, girlfriend, partner

--My mother is a daughter-in-law on the farm, she is still em-
ployed there, I came to the city, but I have no one, only Raquel,
who is the daughter of the owner of the weaving mill, she is my
friend, but her father does not approve of our friendship.

--And then what happens when you get older?

_I worked as a loader in the first factory for a long time, I think
more than 10 years.

_I was fired, the fat old owner of the factory fought with me
and sent me away, I have a lot of back pain, so I went to work in
the other factory, as a cleaner, I live in a small room, a shack in

a kind of garbage dump, further ahead there are other shacks just like it, nobody knows each other, it's dirty...

_How old are you ?

_I'm 35 years old, I've been working here for 8 years...

_ Do you remember how long you were there, or anyone important while you were there?

_ I got sick, I'm hungry, I have a fever, I have pain..., there are some ladies, sisters of charity who take care of me, but I don't think this life will last, I'm very sick.

_Do you want to continue or do you want to stop now?

_Let's continue.

_Don't forget, these are just memories of events that happened a long time ago, nothing will happen to you now in this life. What else do you remember?

_Days and days in bed, I really want to get up, it's raining, there's a leak on top of me...

_What else?

_ I want to close, he said after a while

Right after closing and turning on the lights in the room, he asked me

_What happened, didn't you feel well?

_No, it wasn't that, I was remembering the bed, that whole thing, and I heard a crack, and everything changed, I saw myself outside, a feeling of well-being then everything started to get dark, a strange feeling came, a sadness, so we stopped.

_You died, he said.

_What? What do you mean?

_Well, you were sick in that life and then it came to an end, you just didn't want to remember the post-mortem experience, that's common.

_But that was the end of that stage. I think you got a general overview of it. I want you to think carefully about it, because in the next section we will go to an earlier stage.

_My suffering must have been very great, do I still have a lot to redeem? I'm starting to get scared, you see, I had so much to accomplish in my last incarnation, maybe I still have so much left for this one.

_Not everything in this life is governed by Karma, and Karma is not a checking account either. We all have free will, and that's not all. Just as we have karma, which is the impression of what we must understand in our current existence, we also have the other side of the coin, which is the impression of our potential for achievement, what we can achieve for our spiritual development and that of our brothers and sisters. Unfortunately, this potential is almost always underused, which sometimes leads to terrible consequences. In your case, I think you now have more potential.

_I think it's better if we wrap it up for today Paulo, I think you already have a lot to analyze until next Saturday

When I went to move I realized, my body was, at least it seemed to be, frozen, I couldn't move for a few minutes.

--Alberto, I can't move, my body is stiff

--Don't worry, this numbness will pass, it lasts a little over a minute, start moving little by little, and understand, this is a great sign.

In fact, I started to get up little by little and quickly that passed and I started thinking about having a coffee to finish waking up.

--Explain to me, why is this torpor a good sign?

--This indicates that your brain has immersed itself in the journey to the past, your consciousness has been fully focused on what we were doing and you have reached a level of relaxation that few people achieve.

--Well, I practiced all week to do this.

--Cool, shall we continue next week?

--Sure, I'll come at the same time.

It was already starting to get dark when Alberto went with me to the gate, I went home without seeing Sueli, my work colleague.

Arriving home I went to make dinner because I was hungry, that trip gave me not the tiredness that I imagined would happen, but rather a hunger as if I had done a lot of physical exercise.

At first I couldn't accept that it was really a memory from a previous life, but then what was it? Some creation of my subconscious? Certainly not, because how could I see that old, dusty warehouse with its noisy machines that had appeared in my mind with a certain clarity, as if it were a memory from when I was younger?

That left me impressed, because if in another life I was that janitor, what reason did I have to be him, scum, oppressed, etc. . . , anyway, tomorrow would be another day.

On Sunday, the day dawned a little cloudy, so I went slowly to the bakery near my house to have my coffee, then I returned, Maurício and Carlos soon arrived, they had taken their motorcycles for inspection in a workshop nearby, so they stopped by to talk about the next trip.

--We're thinking about going to Búzios or Arraial do Cabo next Saturday, are you coming with us? Carlos asked.

--I won't be able to attend on Saturday, I'm involved in a project and I can't miss it.

--It's not a new girlfriend because if it were you, you would take her.

--No, it's just a type of exercise.

--What is it, are you working out, at the gym?

--No, it's actually a time travel I'm taking. I said that and had to wait for the laughter to stop, because, of course, they didn't believe me.

--What do you mean, you invented a machine to travel through time and you're going to see what happens next year or what the result of the next election will be?

--Why does everything we do have to need a machine? I asked Carlos.

--I don't know, but you said it was a trip, so I assumed it was in a machine, after all that's what we always do, we travel with our machines.

--Everything we do happens first in our mind, even a machine, someone created it in their mind, then put it on paper and made it into reality, but everything always starts from an idea.

--So this trip only happens in your mind! Said Maurício.

-- Yes, they are memories of past lives, in fact everything has already happened at some point.

--I know how it is, it's past life therapy, there's a hypnotist who makes you remember things from the past and forgotten.

--But it's not quite like that, it's not through hypnosis, at no point was I hypnotized, it's just an exercise, a kind of meditation.

--And you return to the past with this meditation?

--Yes, I have a guide, a person who is a yoga and meditation teacher, he studies this regression method, so I can't miss it.

--The problem is that this can change you! Carlos interrupted.

--What do you mean? I asked.

--This can change you, your way of thinking and seeing the world, it can even be a good thing, but on the other hand, it can be bad too, it's a risk that I don't know if it's worth it.

--But they are just memories that appear to me in images of something that happened many years ago and I'm not even sure if it was really me.

--The main point is what you said, they appear in images, for the brain, it doesn't make much difference.

--I don't understand what you mean.

--I'll explain to you, every time something causes discomfort to the brain, the reaction is somewhat unpredictable and can change your way of thinking and seeing the world because the brain's synapses change, so, even if you say that they are just past memories, they can affect you because, as you said, they are images, and the brain somehow doesn't make a distinction.

--Okay, but I don't understand what you mean by discomfort to the brain, in meditation I am always comfortably relaxed, I don't feel any discomfort, not even a slight headache.

--I don't mean physical discomfort, I mean discomfort in the primary goals of consciousness.

--My goal is to discover some things from the past.

--No, I am not talking about your goals but rather about a set of goals of consciousness, which are seven or eight depending on how you look at the facts.

--And what are these objectives?

--The first goal of consciousness is the effort to be an individual; the second goal of consciousness is sex, that is, the effort for a) the sexual act b) the creation of children; the third goal is the effort for survival through a group; the fourth is the effort for survival through humanity. Every time you in any way harm these goals, your brain reacts by adapting and creating new synapses, which is what generates cognitive dissonance, which is why I said it is dangerous.

--Okay, but that's during brain formation, they say it's up until seven or nine years of age, isn't that right?

--No, this remains for life, until the brain matures, it suffers much more, but throughout life the person can be influenced, you see, this is what sales techniques do, mental manipulation, they mess with these objectives, provoking a reaction that will somehow benefit the manipulator.

--The fact of the advertisements is well-known, but then, does that mean, if I watch a horror film or a violent film, will that influence my mind?

--Yes, it is, it is the engrams, at first the person does not admit it, but they become more reactive, or change their way of thinking, the response is not immediate, it is not like a drug that has a quick effect, but it is a cumulative thing and sometimes given in homeopathic doses.

--You said there are seven or eight objectives, but you only mentioned four, what are the others?

Carlos then picked up the backpack he was carrying, placed it on the table and took out a book, took a quick look at the beginning of the book and spoke.

--I only remember these four because for me they are the most important, but the fifth dynamic is the effort to survive as a life form and through all life forms, that is, the interest in life as such; the sixth dynamic is the effort to survive in the physical universe and with the help of each of its components; the seventh is the drive to survive as a spiritual being; and the drive for survival as infinity is the eighth dynamic.

--And who is the author of this book, is it Reich? I said this referring to Wilhelm Reich.

--No, the author of this one is L. Ron Hubbard, have you heard of him?

--No, never, who was he, a psychoanalyst?

--No, he was a military man and self-taught scholar, he was the father of Scientology.

--I've heard of that, isn't it a religion?

--It is presented as a religion, but in my opinion it was just a way for Hubbard to escape the various processes to which he was exposed.

--What do you mean, why processes.

--Lawsuits, I quickly read his biography, now imagine, the guy created a system that he called dianetics, and with that he came into conflict with all of psychology, the foundations of Freud, Reich and Jung were seriously shaken and with that he must have faced a rain of problems, transforming dianetics into a religion, he was kind of protected from a war that would only harm him.

--Yes, this is common, every time someone moves against the established system the reaction is strong.

--But tell me, have you ever done any regression work? Maurício asked.

--Yes, yesterday was my first day, it was a real trip.

--And what do you hope to gain from this? Do you want to remember that you were a king or something like that?

--No, I didn't even think about it, in fact I just want to contribute to Professor Alberto's studies.

--Then my friend, you are taking a risk for nothing!

Somewhat disappointed, they left that Sunday morning and I was left wondering what danger I was running in my trips to the past. Of course, I wasn't going to take into account what Maurício had said, after all, his life was very different from mine, he had no peace at home and I, on the contrary, was about to avoid leaving the house as much as possible.

The fact is that I really wanted to return to the past because of a dream that had become recurrent, but it wasn't just that, something was pulling me back to the past and I couldn't explain what it was. Besides, I was enjoying the meditation practices and I was also quite used to being alone because since Sandra had died I hadn't had anyone else, a girlfriend or even a hookup. Loneliness became my best companion. Of course, my life became just going from home to work and from work to college and back home. I didn't intend to fight crime on the streets like a superhero, so I was quite satisfied.

It was a sunny Sunday, so I went to the building's parking lot, got on my motorcycle, which I call Cacilda, and we went for a walk on the beaches, ate something similar to lunch, and rode around a bit to enjoy the day. I walked to the center, then came along the embankment and went to the Rodrigo de Freitas lagoon, where I stopped at a vegan restaurant and ate a salad before returning to the apartment and throwing myself on the bed. I remembered that I should have gone to Macaé to see my parents since I hadn't been there for over a month, but that trip will have to wait for next week.

I left Cacilda in the garage and went up to the apartment. When I got there, I was tired and forced to fall into bed with the intention of sleeping, but within a few minutes, images that I had already seen during the regression exercise began to return to my mind. However, the images appeared to me in a more complete form. What I had only seen briefly before, this time I saw the entire field with several spaced olive trees and other young men picking olives. Then I saw the weaving mill where I worked. There was a wooden staircase and an office at the top. I also saw the daughter of the owner of the weaving mill, and I realized that there was something about her that reminded me of Sandra. I can't explain what it was, but who knows, maybe it was her in that passage.

I couldn't sleep, so I got up and went to make some coffee, intending to catch up on my studies and prepare for the next day, when I remembered what Maurício had said: Do you want to remember that you were a king or something like that? And it quickly occurred to me whether all of that wasn't just a projection of my need for my deceased girlfriend, that is, if someday in the distant past that had really happened to me. The answer to my question immediately came to me; next week I'll know the truth. After all, that passage from a simple life, without many details, meant practically nothing; only by continuing could I know something that would confirm what it was.

By the beginning of the evening, I had already reviewed the subjects I was behind on and had nothing else to do, so I decided to meditate. I grabbed all the cushions, pillows, and blankets in the apartment and made a small pile on top of the bed with the intention of lying down and getting as comfortable as possible. I put two pillows under my legs so that I ended up lying down in a similar way to when I was in the armchair in Alberto's living room, almost lying down and I felt like I was floating. After a few minutes lying down without any clothes on, I felt a slight tingling sensation throughout my body. I thought I was going to fall asleep, but I relaxed because if that happened, the alarm clock would call me at 6:00 am for work. However, I didn't fall asleep, but I felt myself entering an altered state of consciousness, the much talked about meditation that many say should not be done lying down.

A bunch of nonsensical thoughts came into my mind, like a bunch of nervous monkeys jumping up a tree, very scared, maybe because of some wild animal. My hearing seemed to have increased and I could even hear the leaves falling from the trees. It took a while for them to get tired and go quiet. The last one was the fear of a robbery at the bank where I worked. Then I realized that it was just a little fear of the situation I was getting myself into. Soon after, they left and the dog barking somewhere I can't even imagine also disappeared and the world fell into a deep silence. But I was still there, aware that I wasn't sleeping, until I decided to get up and realized that it was already past 3:00 in the morning. I was scared because time had passed in a way that I hadn't noticed and I quickly became suspicious that I had slept and not even felt it. I sat on the bed next to the pillows that I had piled up and thought about how I had slept and not noticed it. I was left with doubt, but I had discovered a new practice to explore, an unusual universe within my own mind that no one had ever taught me anywhere.

I lay down again, this time without the pillows making me a shell and I slept quickly, I dreamed again about the pyramid and those people with the strange clothes, this time it was not the same dream, but it seemed to me a continuation of what had been happening, I saw myself outside the pyramid, carrying a heavy leather bag, the red woman did not appear this time, but I somehow realized that she was there in that place, in my mind I was there because of her, so I woke up at 6:00 am with the alarm clock, it was time to have my coffee and leave for work at the bank.

At night, during the class break, I met Maurício. He was with the motorcycles, parked in the parking lot next to the building, so I asked him about the motorcycle. We talked a little about the classes, then I said that I was going to Macaé to see my parents the following Sunday and then I ended up telling him about my recurring dreams. I didn't even mention the trips to the past for fear of his reaction, but he didn't miss the opportunity.

--Paulo, you really want to end up in a mental hospital, don't you!

--Of course not, how could that happen?

--You keep doing those experiments with your mind, remember what Carlos said, that's dangerous.

--Okay, but what does that have to do with the dream I told you?

--It's pretty clear to me, you keep messing with things that are deep in your brain, and you end up having these meaningless dreams, you'll end up going crazy. I think what you really need is to get a girlfriend, exchange energy, you know?

I noticed my friend's concern, but I didn't think he was right. Of course I missed Sandra, but I didn't know anyone who could replace her. She was my companion, for everything, and the girls

I knew simply didn't please me. So I preferred to be alone than to have a girlfriend who didn't meet my expectations or, even worse, who would move in with me and enter my life once and for all, something I didn't want because I was in a phase where I was discovering altered states of consciousness and I could only share this after some time of practice.

--Okay, Mauricio, I'll think about it and see what I can do. I spoke with the intention of ending the matter, but Carlos arrived shortly after.

--Good evening, are you arranging our next trip?

--Well, early Sunday, or maybe late Saturday, I'll go to Macaé to see my parents, maybe I'll return on Monday morning.

--How long is the journey?

--I've never been there by motorbike, but it's about two hundred kilometers away.

--I won't be able to go with you. Said Mauricio.

--I won't be able to go either, my wife wants to go to Angra dos Reis to see a friend and I said I would take her.

Only then did I notice that Carlos was married, in his forties, with some white hair, he even looked like one of the teachers, what united us were the motorcycles that they all had and used constantly.

--Carlos, when you talked about the priorities of the conscious mind, you mentioned seven objectives but forgot one.

--These are the layers of consciousness, and what have I forgotten?

--From the pursuit of pleasure, there must be a layer or a goal as well.

--No, this pleasure thing is already in the subconscious, it is the one responsible for this part. That is why we see so many crazy things that people do in search of pleasure, the subconscious is kind of out of control, and what is worse, in many cases this search is reversed.

--Just like I didn't understand?

--The subconscious for some reason associates psychological suffering with pleasure, so this suffering will occur with a certain constancy in the person's life because the subconscious attracts the things that happen in our life. This is one of the reasons I told you that those experiments are dangerous.

--Carlos, don't take it the wrong way, but is this proven by any scientist, any thesis or something that certifies it, or are you just making this up in your head?

--No, but in practice this is what you will see everywhere, look at people who win prizes, like lotteries, most of them end up in a worse situation than before they won, sometimes the person receives an inheritance that they did not count on and loses everything, or in some cases the person even becomes depressed because nothing goes right in life, for no apparent reason. These are the so-called "limiting beliefs" that people talk about so much.

--I've heard about limiting beliefs, but I don't believe that part about the subconscious that you mentioned is quite like that, the subconscious attracting problems, I can't even imagine how that could be.

--Look, there are limiting beliefs, right? The person believes that they can't perform a certain task and when they try, it goes wrong, right?

--Exactly!

--Now imagine, for example, a person in traffic, who behaves badly, drives faster than normal, doesn't respect other cars and does everything with little attention, what happens?

--Accident, of course!

--It's not just that, from time to time this person will be arguing with someone and will blame fate or the other person or the conditions of the street and who knows what else. So this is what I say, the subconscious attracts these facts because it associates some form of pleasure with it, understand, the subconscious's language is emotion.

--You mean, like the "Law of Attraction"?

--That's right, people believe in the law of attraction to try to attract money and other material things, but they think that the problems they get into are just the work of fate. In fact, taking responsibility is a rare thing these days.

--I understand Carlos, but does this always happen or only with some specific facts?

--I think that's what always happens, people just aren't prepared to recognize it, so they attribute everything to chance, the stars, God or the Devil and everything else you can imagine.

--I have to go, it's time for the last class, we'll talk more about this tomorrow.

So after that conversation I went back to class and then went home. I didn't see Carlos again that week that passed quickly and to my delight, Saturday soon arrived and there I was going to another meeting with Alberto.

And on Saturday afternoon, there I was again with Alberto for another trip to my past, I was afraid that my anxiety would prevent me from relaxing enough, but I hid that fact and went ahead.

-- Okay, sit down and let's get started. Alberto said, pointing to the reclining chair as he closed the window and turned on the light that illuminated the painting.

As I settled into my chair, the familiarity of the surroundings began to calm me, although my body still felt a little tense. I took a deep breath, trying to convince myself that this feeling of anxiety was just a natural reaction to the unknown. Alberto, with his calm and controlled voice, began the relaxation process, leading me back along the path we had taken the week before. Each word he spoke sounded like a mantra, and little by little, I felt my mind begin to detach itself from the hustle and bustle of the present. It was as if an invisible current was pulling me deeper. This time, the process seemed faster, almost as if my body and mind already knew what to expect and were more willing to surrender to that state of tranquility and introspection. The tension gradually dissipated, and the door to my past began to open again.

-- Now I'm going to wait a minute for you to recall last Saturday's exercise, then he continued.

-- I want you to imagine the tunnel and enter it, I'm going to count to ten while you walk towards the light at the end, after this count he asked me.

-- What do you see? Without opening my eyes I answered.

-- A horse, I'm in the stable.

-- And what are you doing there?

-- I'm going to brush the horse. Then I found myself in a large stable with about fifty horses, a very clean clay floor and several uniformed soldiers doing the same thing, I was one of them.

-- And what year are you in this memory?

-- It is the year 1700, and the King is dead, we will have war, we are preparing.

-- I'm going to ask you to go back to the time when you were ten years old in this memory.

-- Yes, . . . I'm ready.

-- And what do you see?

-- I'm in the castle garden playing with Mariana.

-- And who is Mariana?

-- Mariana is King Charles II's cousin, she lives here in the castle and is my friend, I live nearby.

-- Let's fast forward to when you were fifteen in this memory.

-- Yes, . . . I'm ready.

-- What do you do now?

-- We are training shooting, I'm going to the army. I want to marry Mariana.

-- And that's why you're joining the army?

-- Yes, Mariana could not marry a peasant, so I will fight to become a knight of the King and marry her.

-- So let's fast forward this memory to when you were 20 years old.

The silence that followed was profound, almost palpable. I felt my breathing slow as images appeared in my mind, initially blurry and distant, but which soon gained frightening clarity. It was a battle scene, a chaotic scene with the roar of cannons and the screams of desperate men. Soldiers were running everywhere, and I could smell gunpowder and the tension in the air. Smoke enveloped the field, and the colors of their uniforms stood out amidst the whirlwind—especially the vibrant red of some soldiers who were quickly approaching. Suddenly, I found myself face to face with one of them. His gaze was cold and determined, as if he were destined to carry out an implacable mission. Before I could react, I felt the impact of a gunshot. The pain was intense, piercing my body like a lightning bolt, and my legs gave out. I fell to the ground, the world around me spinning as my vision slowly darkened. It was the last image that formed before my consciousness began to return to the room with Alberto.

Gradually, I emerged from that deep state, as if I were returning from a long and strange journey. First, it was the sensation of my body, the texture of the chair beneath me, the light weight of my hands resting on my lap. Then, the sounds around me began to filter in, vaguely, until I found myself back in reality. I slowly opened my eyes, blinking a few times as my vision adjusted to the soft light of the room. Before me, Alberto's psychedelic painting captured my attention. The vibrant colors and abstract shapes seemed to flow in an almost hypnotic way, as if there was still a connection between the world of my visions and the present. The contrast between the chaos of the battle I had just experienced and the serenity of the room was stark, but somehow comforting. It was as if the painting represented the disordered flow of thoughts and memories I had just explored. I took a deep breath, trying to absorb what had just happened.

-- What happened, did something disturb your concentration? Alberto asked me.

-- No, it was just that it ended, there was nothing left, I think that passage ended in a battle, the soldier died.

-- So Mariana lost her suitor.

-- Yes, can we start over? I still want to go further back in time.

-- Unfortunately we can't, we have to stop. And... I was going to tell you this before, but we can't go on.

-- Any problem?

-- Yes, we can't continue today and I won't be able to do this to you anymore, it would be risky to expose you to this again.

-- What do you mean, what risk am I running lying here relaxing?

-- There is a risk of irreversible neurological damage, if it were a hypnosis session you would not have the risk but you would also not remember anything, so because of this I do not do more than three sessions.

-- But I would really like to do more of these regressions, I miss knowing about the past, I think there was something in my past that needs to be corrected or known by me and I have no way of remembering, so I miss it, I get upset about it. When you invited me to do this, you said it was an experiment, now you don't want to do it anymore, why do you want to give up? Alberto, I came to do it trusting you, so if there is any risk, I promise to accept it and not complain, no matter what happens. I said, looking him firmly in the eyes.

Alberto looked away, apparently nervous, stuttered and answered me: -- Do you assume the risks that may occur, do you sign a term assuming the consequences of this?

-- Sure, it will be my problem.

-- So we'll do one more session next Saturday, but just one more and we won't do it anymore, please don't insist.

As I stood up from my chair, an uneasy feeling lingered in my mind. Alberto's reluctance to move forward with some parts of the process seemed disconcerting to me. After all, what could be so complicated about something that, on the surface,_It seemed so simple ? The thought haunted me as I left there and rode my bike towards the beach, with the sea breeze cooling my face. I stopped Cacilda, my faithful companion, and continued walking along the beach. As I walked, I continued to reflect. Perhaps Alberto had come across something he preferred not to share, something involving another client, some incident in the past that had made him hesitant to move forward with me. What could it be? An emotional block? Some negative experience from someone else? Maybe someone got stuck in a memory and had difficulty returning to reality? The idea that perhaps someone had been trapped in a kind of limbo between realities intrigued and frightened me at the same time. My mind wandered between these possibilities as I watched the waves gently breaking on the beach, trying to find some logic in Alberto's reluctance.

As my footsteps deepened into the sand, my determination only grew. What I had seen so far was not enough. Something inside me was crying out for more. It made no sense that my existence was just a series of miserable lives, punctuated by pain and suffering. There was a growing restlessness within me, a kind of silent revolt against the idea that life, in all its past manifestations, could be so cruel and purposeless. Where were the meaningful experiences? The moments of joy, of love, of fulfillment?

Somewhere along the line, I should have experienced something more substantial, more lasting. Perhaps a great love, a memorable achievement, a life that was not marked only by the shadow of loss and pain. This dissatisfaction consumed me, and I knew that if I wanted to discover the truth, I would have to delve even deeper into these regressions. I could not stop until I found something that made sense. It was as if I were on a quest for redemption, for a fragment of happiness lost in the mists of time.

That Monday, the Bank was as busy as ever, with the first movements of the day. Sunlight streamed through the large glass windows, illuminating the partitions that separated the workspaces. But my mind was elsewhere, still immersed in the memories of the last session. As soon as I entered, I saw Sueli in her corner, already busy with papers and reports. She always seemed so focused, but I knew she also understood the nature of these regressions; after all, she and Alberto worked together on many of the experiments. As I approached, my mind was buzzing with questions. I wanted to know what was behind Alberto's decision not to go ahead. There was something I didn't understand, something that didn't fit. As soon as Sueli looked up from her tasks, I got straight to the point, asking what had really happened. Her expression remained neutral, but there was a slight gleam of understanding in her eyes, as if she had already expected that question. She knew as well as I did that Alberto was not the kind of person to give up on something without a strong reason. I needed to understand what was behind that reluctance.

Sueli's corner of the office was a sort of refuge from the chaos of daily activities. Her space, isolated by glass partitions, offered a bit of privacy, but also allowed her to observe everything around her. The large window behind her desk opened up a panoramic view of the busy street, with cars rushing by and people walking quickly to work. The contrast between the calm atmosphere of the office and the frenetic pace outside always caught my attention. Next to Sueli, the bank manager's booth was empty, as usual in the early hours of the morning, since he would only arrive later. It was a more formal space, with heavy furniture and an atmosphere that conveyed seriousness. As Sueli continued with her tasks, I wondered if there was any information she could share with me about Alberto, something that might be beyond my reach, but that she, with her closeness, knew. The environment around me seemed indifferent to my anxiety, but I knew that this conversation could be the first step in finding out what was really going on.

-- Good morning Sueli! She was sitting there wearing a long Indian-style dress as usual. I thought it was a little inappropriate for the occasion, and only then did I remember that she always came to work that way, formal but not too much, appropriate for someone who lived with a Hindu student. Alberto was a reserved and reclusive guy, a yoga and meditation teacher, and I have no doubt that he was something more connected to the Hindu religion, perhaps a Brahmin.

-- Good morning Paulo, Alberto told me that you want to continue with the regressions. She spoke to me in a somewhat serious tone, like someone who wanted to scold me.

-- Yes, I do want to, I wasn't satisfied with what I saw in the past, so I asked him to continue, but he only wants to do one more section and I came to ask him if there is a problem, if he had any annoyance with me or even if the issue is some payment that he didn't charge me and he wants to change that.

-- Payment, Alberto doesn't care about money, he has a very solid heritage abroad, an inheritance from his family in Switzerland, that's certainly not the issue, but there was a case of a student who became a bit, let's say, schizophrenic, I think his mind remained in the past, he didn't return completely, can you imagine?

-- And how many sections did this student do?

-- About four or five, then Alberto decided to stop the experiments, he's afraid it could happen to someone else but he had already arranged it with you.

-- He said he couldn't do it anymore, but I insisted that we continue, so he agreed to do it just one more time and I didn't understand why, I thought it was all so simple that I didn't see a problem, now it's explained, he's afraid.

-- Yes, Alberto is very demanding with his work, so he is concerned that there will be complaints and this will result in losses, or even worse, harm someone. But I have a different opinion, I think that this regression practice is just a guided meditation and cannot cause any harm to the person who does it, but it is his work, so I try not to give my opinion.

-- I understand Sueli, but I really want to do more of this, there are more things I want to discover about my past.

-- He will do it on Saturday, don't worry, I'll see if I can help. Sueli told me.

That night, the college campus was busier than usual. The sound of motorcycles pulling into the parking lot was a familiar symphony to me, and the night wind brought a slight sense of electricity to the air. When I parked my Cacilda, my faithful companion on all adventures, next to another sports bike, something about that green machine caught my attention. The contrast between the deep black of my Cacilda and the vibrant green of the new bike was striking, as if it were some kind of sign of something new, perhaps a worthy competitor or someone who, like me, loved the freedom that those two wheels provided. The helmet hanging next to it, from a brand I knew well, indicated that the owner knew what he or she was doing. "New people in the area," I thought, with a slight smile, imagining that this someone would soon be part of our weekend rides, racing along the roads with the wind as our only limit. With that thought in mind, I walked to the classroom, already curious to know who the new member of our group would be.

At break time, I was in the hallway with Carlos and Maurício who had arrived later and had their motorcycles parked next to mine. There were four sports bikes ready for a beautiful race, which could only happen on another day and we didn't know who the green bike belonged to, when suddenly a Goddess with dark skin and long curly hair came racing out, wearing tight leather pants, a jacket and boots with a heel that made her even taller, 1.80 I imagined, my jaw dropped when I saw her.

-- Good evening, I said as she passed by me, almost bumping into me, but she didn't answer, not even a smile. I stood there watching that perfection leave. She went to the green motorcycle, took her helmet off the clip, shook her long hair and put it on. I froze at that sight. She had certainly done that to provoke me and she had succeeded. Then she stretched out her leg and climbed over the dashboard of the motorcycle and in a quick movement, she got into a riding position in a way that I still don't understand and can't do, so much flexibility. I stood there watching her leave, riding as if she were an experienced racer, and quickly disappeared from sight.

-- He liked the new girl, Maurício told me in an ironic tone, because he had seen her pass by and hadn't even answered me.

-- No, very bad-tempered. I replied.

-- She's an international model, she's in the same class as me, she started today.

-- I think you were the one who liked it! And since you already know something about it, since it started today, we're in the middle of the year.

-- She was transferred, she lived in another country, she is the daughter of an ambassador.

-- See, you already know everything about the Black Goddess and you still ask if I liked it.

-- I admit she's very pretty but she's not my type, you can keep her.

Then I noticed that there was a difference in height between him and her, he being shorter and he must not like that difference, I never thought it was because of the skin color, she was black and he was white with blond hair, besides that, Maurício was a little less handsome, but that was just a detail.

During that week we ended up meeting Marta, the black goddess, she studied in Maurício's class and, in order to get attention, the teacher made her introduce herself to the class on the first day, which is why he knew so much about her. We ended up becoming friends in the first week, a friendship that later turned into a solid and revealing relationship, but let's take it one step at a time.

On Saturday there I was again at Alberto and Sueli's house, as soon as we entered the room where we did the regressions and he taught the classes, Sueli called on his cell phone and asked him to open the gate because she was busy, it was an unexpected visit, so he went there to open the gate.

He quickly returned with the visitor who, as he said, was an old friend he hadn't seen for a long time, a tall man with long white hair and beard, dressed in loose clothing that reminded me of Gandalf from "The Lord of the Rings", even the leather bag he had, but appearances are not always deceiving, that person was so strange.

-- Alberto, I see you're busy, but no problem, I'll wait here, I won't disturb you. Said the strange visitor as he sat down in one of the chairs.

-- Paulo, this is Shanerraiananda, my friend and master, he comes from far away, from the state of Espirito Santo, I'm going to ask Sueli to keep him company while we do our work, just a moment.

-- No, Alberto, let's leave it for another day, I don't want to disturb you. I said that hiding my displeasure, already foreseeing that the regression section would not happen.

-- Paulo, if you don't mind, I'd like to stay and watch you, Sueli already told me about you on the phone, one of the reasons that brought me here was this.

-- I prefer to do it today, Shanerraiananda is just like my brother, he can wait and can help too, for my part, there won't be any problem. Alberto said.

-- Well then, let's do it, that's fine with me!

Having said this, he dimmed the lights as we had done in the other sessions and we began another of my regressions, now assisted by two masters.

Having done the counting and the initial relaxation as we had done the other times, upon leaving the imaginary tunnel after going through the memories already recalled in the other sections...

-- I want you to tell me what you see when you leave the tunnel. Alberto's distant voice echoed in my mind.

-- I see the sea, I'm on a ship.

-- Ship, what is this ship like? Are you traveling for vacation, or work?

-- I live here, I'm a pirate, I'm second under the captain of the ship. It's a wooden boat, it has sails and oars.

-- Do you know what year you are in this memory?

-- 1502! I said the first number that came to mind, without thinking, an image just appeared in my mind with that number and I said it.

-- And who is the captain of the boat?

-- Khair ad Din is our commander, we attacked the Christians in Italy. Then I did some research and found out that he was the pirate Redbeard

-- Do you feel good about what you do? Do you have a partner, family?

-- I feel very good about what I do, I love killing Christians, I consider the crew of the boat as my family.

-- Wait a moment! I told Alberto to wait because images began to appear in my mind, they were images of the robberies that that pirate had carried out.

An image came to me that would have been shocking if I hadn't been in that state of relaxation and submission. In that scene, I had a crew member from the ship we were raiding kneeling on the deck. Others from my crew placed a bench in front of him. Then, those who brought the bench forced him to lie down on it. With one blow, I cut off his head with my sword. It fell off and was quickly picked up by the hair by another pirate who showed it to the crew. He was the captain of the ship. We were terrorizing the crew with the aim of getting them to give us something. Finally, we killed everyone on that ship. Only about three children who were on board escaped in a rowing boat.

After that, images of other atrocities that the pirate had committed still appeared in my mind. In one of them, I cut off both hands of a priest who was on board another boat that we had raided and set on fire during the assault.

Those shocking scenes were interrupted by Alberto's voice asking me if we could continue.

-- Besides living at sea and killing Christians, what else did you do during this passage?

Then I remembered being with two others from my group, walking in a city, everything very rustic and dirty, suddenly a group of guards surrounded us and arrested us, we were taken to a building and locked in cells, the population watched our arrest, I thought someone had recognized us and reported us to the guards, but I couldn't understand how that happened.

-- I don't do anything else, all that comes to mind are images of the pirate's life. I answered Alberto, although I wanted him to delve deeper into that exploration, I wanted to know more about those images that appeared in my mind as if it were a film when he said:

-- Try to remember something else about this passage, I'll wait a while for you to remember and tell us.

Then I saw that I was on a kind of platform in a square, next to me were the other two pirates who were arrested with me, the local population was all gathered to watch the event that would be our hanging, a beautiful young woman caught my attention, she must have been about fifteen years old, she kept looking at me fixedly and I returned that look, she stood very close to the platform, her blue eyes somehow were not strange to me, that was the last scene that came to my memory along with a name, Sandra.

-- If you do not wish to explore further, or if there is nothing more to explore from this passage, let us end this regression, I ask you to return to your normal state of consciousness, follow my counting, 5; . . . 4; . . . 3; . . . 2; . . . 1. Is this okay? Can I turn on the lights?

Alberto then turned on the lights in the room and turned off the light that illuminated the psychedelic painting. I returned the chair to its normal position and saw that in front of me, sitting in another chair, was Master Shanerraiananda.

-- Welcome back to the present, did you find what you were looking for? The master asked.

-- No way, with each session we do, more questions and doubts come to mind.

-- Yes, but as we agreed, this was the last one. This could really hurt you and I don't want you to suffer the consequences.

-- Yes I know, what can I do?

-- What do you mean, what can I do? Asked the old master.

-- It's just that I have a curiosity, I say curiosity so as not to use the word need, to know about my past lives, since my girlfriend died this curiosity started to grow in me and I try in every way to know how these passages were, Alberto initially helped me but now he doesn't want to continue anymore, he's afraid that I won't return from the past and will turn into a zombie.

The master placed his hand over his face, covering his eyes in a gesture showing his disappointment.

-- I have a student who went through this process and some problems appeared, he became a bit schizophrenic and I don't want that to happen again. Alberto said.

-- It certainly wasn't because of you, said the master, he must have already had this problem and you hadn't noticed it yet, it came to the surface after some regression, but it could have been at another time, there might even have been no regression and he appeared with the problem, it has nothing to do with you.

-- But I will help you, I will solve your problem.

-- Thank you, and how are you going to do that?

-- Write down your address for me and I will send you an alchemical elixir by mail. Just follow the instructions I will tell you and you will achieve your goal.

The master said that, took a notebook and a pen out of his bag and gave it to me to write down the address. I wrote down my address and wondered, does he have a phone number to write down in memory? I had never written down my address for someone to send me a letter.

-- And what is this alchemical elixir like, is it very alcoholic? I asked, thinking it could be an alcoholic drink or something similar.

-- Because it is alchemical, it is very concentrated, you should use a dropper and use just one drop dissolved in a glass of water at a time, you set aside two to three hours to meditate and then drink the solution and your memories of past lives will return to your mind.

-- And how much will this elixir cost me? I asked the old man, already imagining some scam that I certainly wouldn't fall for.

Alberto looked shocked and left, somewhat indignant, climbing the stairs that led to the other part of the house. I don't know if it was because of my question or the old man's offer, but the old master didn't even show any reaction. He put his hand on his chin and thought for a moment, then answered me.

-- That will cost you half your salary.

-- Thank you, but I can't spend that part of my salary to do that.

-- I know you don't, but I don't want to receive anything, I want you to donate half of your salary to charity after using it, if you have any results, but remember-- only if you have a positive result, otherwise you can return the elixir to Alberto.

I was scared by that situation, he didn't want to receive anything, and since I was going to prove that I had donated some money to charity, I didn't know what to say after hearing that unexpected proposal.

Soon after Alberto returned and asked the master.

-- So, did you come to an agreement?

-- Yes, I proposed an experiment to Paulo, actually a kind of challenge, if the elixir doesn't work, he will return it to you without paying anything, but if it works he will donate a sum of money to charity.

Alberto smiled, finding the situation funny, I took advantage of their relaxed mood to leave and got up to leave, wondering if I should first ask what charity this was, some institution or group, but as I didn't believe it, thinking it was just idle talk, I decided to stay silent, said goodbye to them and left, already thinking about going for a walk along the beach.

Since I was in the Gávea neighborhood, I went to the nearest beach, followed by Leblon beach, parked at Cacilda in a parking lot near Posto 9, hung up my helmet and walked calmly along the beach promenade to clear my mind because I needed to clear my thoughts after those images came to mind. But the scene of the girl looking at me during the hanging, I couldn't accept it. I don't know why that made me uncomfortable, a strong feeling that there was something else there that I hadn't noticed. When I felt a shock in my arm, it wasn't a bad feeling or something that scared me, but a shock of pleasure that I hadn't felt until then. I stopped to look and see what had happened and there she was, Marta had touched me and I felt that unexpected shock. I didn't know what to say for a moment. She was wearing the kind of clothes that women wear to go to and from the beach, her hair tied up and wearing flip-flops, very different from the woman I saw leaving on a motorcycle at college.

-- Good afternoon! She said to me.

-- Hello, good afternoon, you scared me, I came to walk in a different place, I always walk around Copacabana, but today I was passing through and decided to stop here, it's quieter here.

-- I saw you when you stopped the motorcycle and then crossed the street very distracted, is everything okay with you?

-- Yes, it is, and speaking of motorcycles, where's yours?

-- I leave it at home, I live nearby and I walk to the beach.

So we went to the kiosk and I ordered coconut water, we sat down and drank and talked about the motorcycles, about the beach where she came whenever she could, then she started talking about herself, that she was a photo model, but she really liked her privacy and that on her first day at college the professor made her introduce herself to the whole class and that for her it had been an ordeal and she left class at the first opportunity.

Then I reminded her:

-- In college, the first time you passed by me, I said to you, Good night, and you passed by like a hurricane, not even a hello.

-- Oh, I'm sorry, I was very upset because something had happened that I didn't like at all.

-- Wow, that sucks, right on your first day. I hope you got over it and everything is okay now.

-- Yes, these are things of the past, let's leave that behind.

I noticed that we had already started to feel empathy for each other, it was as if we had known each other for many years, of course I really wanted to be with her, but that attraction went far beyond that, I avoided thinking that I had found the woman I had always looked for, but she was right there in front of me and I didn't know what to do when she suddenly...

-- Look, it's already getting dark, I'm going home to take a nice shower, eat something, rest.

-- Resting, on a Saturday night, for sure. I asked if I would do anything different, in fact I always stayed locked up at home and sometimes I would go out the next day to ride my motorcycle, go to Macaé to see my parents or take a trip to the mountains.

-- If you don't have any plans, you can come with me, then we can go out, what do you think? When she said that I didn't believe it, she was asking me to go to her house, and then go out.

-- Sure, let's go. I got up, paid the bill at the kiosk and we went to get the motorcycle that was parked a few meters away from where we were.

She told me the way, it was on Vinícius de Moraes Street, which is just a few meters from where the motorcycle was parked, on the second block, an old building with a garage downstairs, facing the street, there was an intercom at the entrance to the garage, she called the concierge and asked them to open the gate so I could park the motorcycle there next to her machine, then we went up in the elevator that left the garage itself and went to the apartment where she lived, I was already thinking that at the first meeting I would find her mother or parents, but when she opened the door there was only a cat on the sofa in the living room.

The apartment was medium-sized, and in the living room there was a wall on the side of the entrance with a kind of photo mural, several pictures of her, most of them black and white photos and in the center a color poster of her kneeling in the sand on a beach, a beautiful photo, I thought "she must be a narcissist", she turned on the television and asked me to wait while she took a shower, I stayed there in the living room waiting, I also noticed that in another corner there was a table with a computer and some fashion magazines, diaries, only work stuff, at the back of the room a window where you could see the street above the many trees there, I sat on the sofa, the cat went out and I waited for almost an hour for her.

After all this waiting, she came to be with me, dressed in a white robe. I stood up and as soon as I got close to her, she hugged me and gave me an exciting kiss, in which I felt her perfume and the taste of mint on her lips. We were completely relaxed when the intercom rang, interrupting us. She went to answer it. It was the doorman, announcing that there was another motorcycle next to hers. She had to explain to the doorman that everything was fine, that she had placed it there, and then she hung up. At that moment, I remembered that there were people watching her and that she was not in a place where there was no care, where she was a stranger. We kissed again. We ended up in the bedroom after a few hours of intense and delicious sexual activity.

-- Do you still want to go out or would you rather stay here? Marta asked me with the most cynical face she could make at that moment. I answered that I would rather stay but that after all that I was hungry, so we ordered dinner for us at a Japanese restaurant. I also ordered a wine that I already knew. We spent that first night together, and so we continued to have fun in a way that made clear the mutual need we felt, since we had both been without company for longer than we would have liked.

On Sunday morning, I woke up and without thinking I spoke.

– Oh, I have to go! Marta, who was already awake next to me, rolled over in bed and got on top of me, speaking in a very affectionate voice, softly in my ear.

-- I forbid you to repeat those words!

-- Forbidden, what do you mean?

-- Never say that to me again, never say you're leaving.

-- But I thought about going home to change my clothes, to see if everything is okay, after all tomorrow will be another day of work.

-- Going home is one thing, you may need it, but saying you're going away hurts. Know that words have power, when you say it, you open the possibility of it happening.

-- So, how should I speak?

-- I guess you could say, "Let's go to my apartment."

-- Okay then, let's go out and stop by my apartment.

So we left, got on the motorcycles and rode along the beach until we reached the street where I lived. On the way I thought, how long had I been with Marta? 2 or 3 years? No, it would have been 24 hours since we were together and she had already told me that words have power. I really needed to know more about her, about the philosophy she had in her mind, her principles, her beliefs and maybe some religion. But my feeling was that I had known her for a few years because I felt extremely good by her side and I knew that that weekend was coming to an end, but we would meet at college on Monday night.

When we arrived at the building where I lived, we did the same routine: call the concierge, open the basement, put away the two machines, and go up to the small apartment where I lived, which was smaller than hers. That's how we ended that Sunday, cuddled together on my bed, not wanting to let go of each other.

The following week began with a light rain, the kind that seems more like a lament than a change in the weather. It was a persistent, almost constant drizzle that permeated the air with a gentle melancholy. This weather, however, made my routine more challenging. Cacilda, my faithful motorcycle, had always been my companion on adventures around the city, but riding through the muddy and congested streets of Rio de Janeiro on rainy days required not only attention, but an extra dose of courage. The traffic in Rio, already chaotic on normal days, became a veritable Russian roulette with the wet road. In addition, there was no shortage of puddles of dirty water, and some inattentive or even ill-intentioned driver would always end up forcing me to drive over them, drenching me in mud and city debris. That light but persistent rain seemed to refuse to let up, remaining firm until Thursday, as if it were an additional character in my week.

During this time, Marta had stayed in my bed, and we had arranged to meet at college, which became a new source of excitement in my routine. Being with her seemed to transform even the darkest days. After two long years of living without a relationship, without a person by my side, having to face the challenges of everyday life alone, Marta had appeared in my life with the force of a whirlwind. There was something so natural between us, as if we had known each other for years. We had countless similarities, and this brought a comforting feeling, a kind of companionship that I didn't even know I missed so much. There were no ghosts from the past haunting our relationship; no ex-girlfriends to worry about or comparisons to make. Dropping her off at my apartment in the morning, without any hesitation or concern, was proof of this.

She arrived at the college later than agreed, as usual, since I always had the habit of arriving early due to my work. We only met at the end of class. I was already in the hallway, near where we usually parked our motorcycles, watching the line of motorcycles with hers right there, next to mine. I felt a silent relief when I saw her bike among the others. The rain, which had previously threatened to continue, had given a brief respite when Marta, with her typical lightness, approached me softly. She wrapped her hands around my shoulder, without me noticing her arrival, and almost instinctively pressed her body against my left side. The gesture was intimate, and her voice, when she spoke, was soft like the breeze that precedes a storm.

-- Okay? Can we leave?

Her calm and affectionate manner contrasted with the intensity of my feelings at that moment. Without thinking, I returned her gesture with a tender kiss and replied that yes, it was time for us to leave. That moment, although routine, remained etched in my mind in a striking way. Something about that scene seemed familiar, as if I had experienced it before, and then I remembered my dream that had been recurring. In it, a woman in a pyramid placed her hands on my shoulder in the same way that Marta had just done. Although it was just a coincidence, I couldn't help but think about the strange connection between the two figures. Despite the obvious physical differences between Marta and the woman in the dream, the gesture was identical, and this planted a seed of curiosity and uneasiness in my mind.

Keeping up with Marta on her motorcycle was a challenge in itself. She rode with the skill of someone who seemed born for it, and I, with all my experience, had to work hard to keep up with her. We headed towards Ipanema, and when we arrived in front of her building, she pulled the motorcycle into the parking lot, while I stood at the entrance, a little lost as to what I should do next. We hadn't made any plans beyond the route we had shared.

-- Come in too, stay here with me – Marta said with a smile. – I need a ride to the airport tomorrow morning.

I accepted the invitation without hesitation, and we went up to the apartment. As we rode in the elevator, a part of me wondered why she needed to go to the airport, but my curiosity was soon satisfied. Marta explained that she had to catch the first flight to São Paulo for an important job, and that she would be back the same day. I agreed to take her, and I felt a small sense of satisfaction in being able to help her with something so important.

At the apartment, she prepared a simple but delicious dinner. With every conversation, every smile, I felt our connection grow stronger. We spent the night together, the atmosphere between us was light and passionate. In the morning, we left for the airport before sunrise, and I left her there with a quick kiss, staying to watch the plane take off. I watched until it disappeared over the horizon, and then I went back to my apartment.

When I got home, I was pleasantly surprised. Everything was tidy, the dishes were washed, and the kitchen was spotless. I remembered that on Monday, I had left Marta in bed and rushed off to work. That touch of organization made me realize how her presence had already impacted my life in subtle but profound ways. For the first time in a long time, the apartment had a welcoming air, with a feminine touch that I didn't know I was missing. Marta had entered my life with the same ease with which she rode her motorcycle—fast, decisive, and at the same time, comforting. And, without realizing it, I was already starting to like it.

The rest of the day dragged on, perhaps because I was so impatient to see her again. When I finally got to college, I parked my motorcycle and got ready for another night of classes. A few minutes later, my phone rang. It was Marta, telling me that her work in São Paulo had taken longer than expected and that she would only be back on Thursday. I felt a chill in my stomach when I heard her words, as if a bucket of ice water had been poured over me. That empty feeling made me realize that I was already more involved with her than I had imagined. The feeling was clear: I was starting to fall in love.

At least I rode my motorcycle home more calmly. The night was silent, interrupted only by the light sound of the drizzle that was starting to fall again, running down the streets and forming small streams on the sidewalks. I arrived at my apartment with my mind full of thoughts that I couldn't organize. I took a hot shower, but the water, instead of relieving the weight on my shoulders, didn't seem to be enough to cleanse the restlessness inside me. I decided to call Marta. Even without having anything specific to say, the simple act of hearing her voice calmed me down. It was as if, through the phone, I could touch a piece of her presence, as if that invisible thread that connected us was enough to dispel the loneliness that was beginning to swirl around.

When she answered, I felt an immediate sense of relief. We talked for almost an hour, although I didn't really know what to talk about. Marta, on the other hand, was full of news. She told me enthusiastically that the reason she had come to São Paulo was to audition for a modeling agency. The people at the agency had been impressed with her, and her chances of getting a new job were very good. Her enthusiasm was contagious, but inside, I began to feel a slight anxiety, like a dark cloud gathering in the distance. What if she actually got the job? What if she had to travel frequently? As she talked about her plans, I began to question what this meant for us. We had barely started and I was already wondering how we would maintain this relationship if she spent more time away from Rio. When the conversation finally came to an end, we said goodbye. She needed to rest, because the next day promised to be full.

I hung up the phone, but the silence that filled the apartment again did not bring the peace I had hoped for. Instead, it brought a wave of insomnia that made me walk to the window, where I sat down to watch the rain fall outside. The darkness of the city seemed to reflect the emptiness I was beginning to feel. I stood there, lost in my thoughts, as the drops of water ran down the glass. A silent sadness hit me. The truth, which until then I had been trying to ignore, finally became clear: I was needy. After two years of living alone, since Sandra's death, I had become accustomed to loneliness. It was an irritating but familiar companion. I had grown accustomed to my own company, without sharing my time or space with anyone else. But now, after just three days with Marta, my world had changed. Everything was different, and I no longer knew if I was ready to deal with it.

I woke up the next morning around four o'clock, before the sun had even risen. There was an uncomfortable emptiness inside me, as if something essential was missing, something I couldn't name. What had once felt comfortable—my solitude—was now starting to bother me. Maybe I was getting used to being alone. I got up, unable to go back to sleep, and got dressed. I grabbed Cacilda and went for a walk around the city. The early morning air was cold, biting my skin, but somehow it made me feel more present, more alive. Driving through the still-sleeping city was almost therapeutic. The streets were slowly coming to life, with the first lights coming on in the stores and street vendors carrying their stalls to their points of sale.

It seemed like the world was waking up, but my mind was still lost in a maze of reflections. I stopped at a traffic light, and even when it changed, I remained there, as if trapped in a bubble of thoughts. The light changed, then changed again, and I remained standing, watching the street vendors arriving and starting their daily struggle. The image of them, carrying their junk, brought to mind the regressions to past lives that fascinated me so much. Those faces, full of weariness and resignation, seemed to reflect an endless cycle of suffering and struggle for survival. It was as if they were trapped in an endless wheel, life after life, trying to survive without great rewards. And then, I thought about my own past lives. In how many of them had I also struggled, suffered, made terrible mistakes? The pirate I had been killed without remorse; the cleaner at the weaving mill had died in total abandonment, without anyone caring. It was the same consciousness that dragged itself through time, but I knew that I was no longer the same person.

These thoughts stayed with me until I stopped at a café next to the bank where I worked. I went in to have my breakfast, still lost in thought. The clerk, his eyes heavy with tiredness, came to serve me and said something about the Flamengo game that would take place on Wednesday. I was so far away that I barely registered his words, I just nodded, not knowing exactly what to say. It was as if we were in different worlds: he was worried about football, and I was immersed in questions about the past and the nature of human suffering. I drank my coffee in silence and went on to another day of work.

The day at the bank dragged on slowly. Even though I kept busy during my lunch break, time seemed frozen, as if the hours refused to pass. When I finally left, a little later than usual, I decided to go straight home. Despite all the changes that were happening in my life, I knew that I would not give up on my project of investigating the past. Missing classes that night would not be an irreparable loss. On the way, I went down to Ipanema beach. I walked along its entire length, watching the waves crash against the sand, as if they were trying to tell me something that I was not yet able to understand. Then I passed in front of Marta's apartment before returning to my own. The emptiness inside me persisted, but now it was accompanied by a determination: I had to continue investigating my past lives, even without Alberto to guide me.

When I got home, I decided to stop by the supermarket and buy a pizza. The idea of cooking anything was far from my plans. All I wanted to do was spend the rest of the night meditating, trying to reconnect with those old memories, those lives that seemed so distant, but at the same time so present in my consciousness.

After settling into the couch, I picked up the phone and called Marta. The phone rang several times, but she didn't answer. I waited a few minutes, staring out the window, and tried again. The silence that returned after each unanswered ring began to unsettle me. After half an hour, I called a third time, but still nothing. The night seemed to be stretching out, and all I could do was wait for her to call me back. I sat by the window, watching the dim streetlights, and prepared myself to face another night amidst my own memories.

I got home and, anxious, called Marta. The phone rang incessantly until the line dropped. She didn't answer. Impatient, I went to the window and began to observe the street, the dim lights of the streetlamps and the few cars passing by. The silence of the night seemed to amplify my restlessness. After half an hour, I tried to call again, but the result was the same. I waited a little longer, trying to shake off my nervousness, and made a third attempt, without success. The only thing left for me to do was wait for the calls to be returned, but, to my frustration, that didn't happen that night.

Feeling helpless in the face of the situation, I decided that the best thing to do was to try to distract my mind. I arranged the pile of pillows, as I had done on another occasion, and leaned back to meditate. I wanted to somehow relive the experience I had had with Alberto. I closed my eyes, took a deep breath, and tried to relax. I concentrated, visualizing the time tunnel again, but every time I tried to move forward, something would break my concentration. Maybe it was the restlessness that was taking over me, a lack of inner peace. I tried several times, but I couldn't get into the necessary state of tranquility. In the end, tiredness got the better of me and I ended up falling asleep.

On Wednesday morning, I was awakened by the insistent ringing of the phone. It was Marta. She immediately apologized for not answering the phone the night before. She explained that her cell phone had run out of battery and that was why she couldn't call back. I accepted her apology, trying to appear understanding, but inside, anger and jealousy were eating away at me. I wanted to pour out everything I felt, complain and tell her exactly what was bothering me, but I held back my emotions. It was the first time this had happened, so I thought it would be better to talk to her in person. After all, she would be back on Thursday.

Changing the subject, I asked about her cat. I was curious to know what she did with the animal while she was away. Marta explained that she left the cat in the care of her aunt, who lived in the apartment next door. I took the opportunity to cut the conversation short. I said that I had to get ready for work and we hung up. That phone call made me even more uneasy. Although I accepted the explanation, something inside me remained suspicious. Even so, I continued with my routine, since it was time to leave.

Later, before leaving for college, Marta called me from São Paulo. Her voice was full of enthusiasm. She asked if I could pick her up at the airport that evening. She was thrilled because she had managed to change her ticket and would be returning to Rio on the 9:00 p.m. flight. I arranged everything and, at the end of the day, I went to the airport to meet her.

I parked Cacilda and headed to the arrivals area. A short while later, I saw on the board that the flight was arriving. I waited anxiously, and soon Marta appeared, walking towards me with quick steps. When she saw me, her eyes lit up and she hugged me tightly, still in the middle of the aisle. It felt like we hadn't seen each other in weeks, even though it had been a short trip. Her enthusiasm was contagious. She told me that everything had been a success at work, and we had dinner right there, at the airport, before heading to her apartment.

As soon as we entered, she looked at me with a mischievous smile and, without hesitation, said:

— Shall we go to the beach?

I looked at her, surprised. "Tomorrow is Thursday, and I have to work at the bank, remember?"

— Yes, but I want to go now. Shall we?

I glanced at my watch. It was just after 10 p.m. It wasn't cold, and the sky was clear, but the idea of going to the beach at that hour seemed strange. Plus, I was still in my work clothes. Still, she convinced me. Her smile was irresistible. She quickly changed into something more comfortable and pulled me outside.

Arriving at the beach, Marta ran to the sand, full of energy, and spread a towel on the ground, as if it were a sunny day. Before I could say anything, she ran towards the sea and dove in, the waves gently lapping against her body. I stood there, perplexed, not quite understanding this sudden change in behavior. She returned to the beach soon after, still wet, with her hair dripping, and kissed me, laughing.

"I've been dying to do this," she said, satisfied. "Now we can go back. I've satisfied my desire."

Suddenly, all the lights around us went out. The entire neighborhood, perhaps the city, was in darkness. Only the headlights of the cars passing by on the avenue provided any light. Marta looked up, and I followed her. The sky, now free of light pollution, revealed stars that we were not used to seeing.

"Look, it's the Hunter," she said, pointing to the constellation Orion. A strange peace came over us. It was as if the universe had suddenly conspired to make us live that unique moment under the stars.

-- Yes, I have seen it. I said as I looked up at the stars.

-- I came from there!

-- What do you mean, you're an alien?

-- No, I was born here on Earth, but I've already lived on a planet there.

-- A planet in the Betelgeuse system?

-- No, from the star Rigel!

-- I don't know which one it is, but how do you know it came from there? I spoke and the streetlights returned, making it difficult to see.

-- It's an intuition of mine, I feel a kind of nostalgia every time I look there, I think I've already lived some lives here, then I lived there and for some reason I returned to this world, to learn something

-- Or pick up something you left here.

-- One day we'll go out to a place where we can see more clearly and I'll show you where it is.

-- I know some places that must be really good for seeing the sky at night. On the way up to Teresópolis there is a viewpoint where you can see a lot, but I've never spent the night there. We can go there on Saturday.

Her idea seemed irresistible. A quiet place, away from the city lights, where we could observe the sky more clearly. I nodded with a smile, already imagining the scene. After this brief moment of contemplation, we returned to Marta's apartment. The night passed quickly, and in the morning, after a quick coffee, I left for work, already arranging to meet later at the college.

Saturday finally arrived, and we set off on a motorcycle ride. We decided to go to the Soberbo viewpoint, on the road to Teresópolis, about 120 kilometers away. The winding road that cut through the mountains was stunning, surrounded by dense and lush vegetation. We arrived at the viewpoint while the sun was still high in the sky, illuminating the vast expanse of forest, the imposing rock formations of the Serra dos Órgãos and the city of Guapimirim, spread out on the plain at the foot of the mountains. The view was breathtaking.

After admiring the scenery for a while, we decided to head into town and wait for nightfall. We were eager to see the starry sky, which promised to be spectacular. We stopped at a small, cozy café overlooking the mountains, where we ordered two hot coffees. The sun was beginning to set, painting the horizon with warm, soft colors, promising a clear, cloudless night. Everything seemed perfect.

As we sipped our coffee, Marta picked up her phone to check a message that had just arrived. Her face, which had previously been relaxed and smiling, suddenly changed. She read the message silently and then leaned back in her chair. Her eyes, now fixed on me, expressed a mixture of indecision and discomfort.

— What happened? — I asked, noticing the strange atmosphere that had formed between us. It took her a few seconds to answer, which increased my curiosity even more.

— I need to ask you something — She began, her voice softer than usual.

— Can I store my motorcycle in your apartment's garage for a few days?

I was surprised by the question, but I didn't see any problem with it.

— Of course you can, no problem. But why are you asking me this now?

She gave a light sigh before continuing.

— I was just thinking... I don't know if I want to go back to Rio today. I thought we could spend the night here, find somewhere quiet to stay, and come back tomorrow.

The idea of spending the night in the mountains sounded nice, especially after all the scenery we had already enjoyed so far. I quickly agreed.

— Great! We can find a hostel and spend the night here. Tomorrow we'll go back to Rio without rushing.

Marta smiled, but there still seemed to be something worrying her.

— Okay, we'll do that, but I really need to leave the bike in your garage for a few days. Maybe a week...

The way she avoided looking directly at me as she spoke intrigued me. Something was going on, but I didn't want to press her at that moment.

— It's okay, Marta. Leave the bike there for as long as you need — I replied, trying to reassure her, but inside my mind was starting to spin with questions.

That brief conversation, as the sun disappeared over the horizon, planted a seed of uneasiness in me. Was there something more behind this request? Trying to push my thoughts away, I smiled at her and suggested that we quickly find a place to spend the night. I didn't want to spoil the mood of this getaway that had started off so well.

-- Are they doing work on your building some days?

-- There is no construction work, but my mother is arriving there today and she doesn't know that I own a motorcycle. If she only sees the motorcycle in the garage, as she has already seen, I'll tell her it belongs to a neighbor, but she can't see me arriving home riding a motorcycle, or with a helmet in my hand. She has some trauma regarding motorcycles.

I had to laugh a little at that situation, after all, owning a motorcycle "hidden" from my mother as if she were some child, an independent, professional woman, in good health and in perfect physical condition, seemed like an exaggeration to me.

-- You're laughing because you don't know what I've been through with my mother and her crazy antics! Marta spoke to me in a more severe tone than usual, a fact that immediately put me out of humor because I realized that among the many things we had in common, we had problematic mothers. And she continued with her complaint.

-- I have that apartment and my aunt lives next door but she thinks I live with my aunt, and that the apartment is just a kind of office, that I don't sleep there.

-- But if the apartment is yours, what does it have to do with her?

-- The apartment is mine, my father gave it to me, he bought it many years ago when he worked in Rio, then he returned to Angola and rarely comes to Brazil.

-- So your father is Angolan, your mother too?

-- No, she is from the interior of Alagoas and lives there in Maceió but because of their separation, she thinks the apartment is hers.

-- And your Aunt, what does she say about this?

-- My aunt Marina is the one who helps me contain the beast, if it weren't for my aunt I don't even know what would have happened, my mother has a lot of problems and thinks I'm responsible for some of her incompleteness.

-- I know how this kind of thing is, I barely talk to my mother, she has always been very narcissistic, very selfish, so I don't even talk about my problems with her. My father lives only for his company, whenever he has a break he disappears somehow to avoid trouble.

-- So it's a failed marriage?

-- Yes, they don't talk about it, but they each live their own lives and I don't notice any kind of affection between them, they are like two strangers living at the same address, and they even sleep in separate beds.

-- My aunt Marina has a friend who has an enviable relationship with a guy who has been married for 45 years and they are always making plans, traveling everywhere and seem to always be dating, I think this is the result of each person's mental preparation.

-- I don't understand, what do you mean by mental preparation?

-- When I talk about mental preparation, I mean the mental programming we received when we were still young and our minds were still forming, this programming that gives rise to our self-image, what we see of ourselves in the world, or the mental projection of the most hidden boxes of the subconscious that define everything we are, which is why there are problems that persist in our families, such as separations, dissatisfaction with life, you can see there are things that your father couldn't do, your mother couldn't do, your grandparents couldn't do, some call it family karma. If you believe, like me, in reincarnations, living one life and then repeating the same mistakes in another life is actually true torture.

-- The same thing happens with people who have a mental programming of scarcity, no matter how much money they earn, they will always be complaining and returning to need.

-- True, I have to agree with you on that, I always say that there are two angels, the angel of abundance and wealth and the angel of poverty and scarcity, but deep down that's exactly it.

-- Isn't there something wrong there? Because wouldn't the "angel" of poverty and scarcity be the demon of poverty and scarcity?

-- Not at all, think about it, both serve to teach us about life's problems, poverty teaches us to share the little we have, it teaches us humility and temperance, in short, it teaches us to value what we have achieved, that's why I say it's an angel and not a demon.

-- I see, and what's wrong with your mother that she's so problematic?

-- When my mother was a child, she lost her father, my grandfather, in a motorcycle accident and she saw everything because she was in a car that was following right behind on the road, so she can't stand the idea of seeing me on a motorcycle, once she saw me with a boyfriend on a motorcycle, she made a scene, got sick, and ended up in the hospital with a heart attack.

-- Wow, how sad! But it's already dark enough, shall we go to the lookout point to see the sky?

So we left the café, got on our bikes and went to the viewpoint. In about 15 minutes we got there and parked our bikes side by side at a suitable stop at the viewpoint. Near us there were other people with cars parked looking at the sky and the plain below. It was a beautiful, warm night with a stunning view of the stars. Leaning against Cacilda, I hugged Marta and we looked at the sky. We were soon able to see the constellation of the hunter, when she showed me the star Rigel. With a slightly emotional voice, she spoke.

-- I'm sure I've lived in that place before

-- And do you think that because you feel like an alien or have some memory of a past life there?

-- In my case, it's just a feeling of nostalgia that I feel when I look there, I have no memory and I don't think I'm an extraterrestrial, do you think it's impossible that there's life there?

-- No, I don't think it's impossible, I even think it's very likely that there's another civilization there, what I don't believe is that there's a possibility of a being from there coming here, I think that God separated the worlds with all that distance precisely so that they would never meet.

-- For a person who doesn't believe in any religion, how do you talk about God? Marta told me in a somewhat sarcastic tone.

-- It is one thing to believe in God, another thing to believe in religions, all of which were created by "human men".

-- And you, what do you believe in besides aliens?

-- What do you mean, what do I believe in?

-- Yes, what is true for you, people always believe in something, some believe in prophets, gurus, the Pope, reincarnation, money, and you?

-- For me, the truth is sex; sex is the truth, because a woman or a man can fake an orgasm, but no one can feel an orgasm and say it was nothing, because they would be lying to themselves. So this is because the orgasm occurs within the mind, and when the body dies, what remains? Only the mind remains. So the highest astral is a pure orgasm, a place where you feel this constantly. When the mind is not tied to the hell it created in life, tied to material things and suffering because it cannot enjoy those things, it is in pure pleasure.

God created all things through sex, in everything that exists there are two sexes, the positive and the negative side, one does not exist without the other.

-- Yes, even batteries have a positive side and a negative side.

-- All matter that exists was manifested in this way, when nothing existed, the subatomic particles united and from this conjunction atoms emerged, so Paulo, understand that it is this energy that creates and maintains the worlds I am talking about, this is the purest truth, religions are just human inventions.

-- Imagine this, this thought of yours in the Middle Ages people would kill each other without thinking twice

-- What thought?

-- That heaven, the highest astral is a pure orgasm.

I said this and, at that moment, it seemed like everything around us disappeared. The stars, once so bright and present in the sky, became just a distant memory. The magic of the moment enveloped us, and the kiss we had begun replaced any other concerns with a growing desire to be together, comfortable, far from any rush or commitment. The original plan was to enjoy the end of that Saturday in a relaxing way, but, without having made reservations at hotels or guesthouses along the way, reality knocked on the door. We then decided that the best thing would be to return home, which, luckily, was only 100 km away. In that context, this distance seemed like just an extension of our adventure, a final touch to a night that had already been special.

We chose the quieter route, crossing the Rio-Niterói bridge, which offered magnificent views of the city lights reflecting on the dark waters. The evening wind caressed our faces as the bikes glided smoothly over the asphalt, making the journey even more pleasant. In just over an hour, we were back, storing our bikes in the apartment garage. The feeling of satisfaction for a day well spent still hung in the air.

The next morning, Marta got ready early for an important appointment with her mother. While she got ready, the silence between us seemed comfortable, a reflection of the complicity we had. I accompanied her to the building's lobby, enjoying every second with her before she went on her way.

As I was saying goodbye and getting ready to go back up to the apartment, the doorman, with a discreet gesture, called me. "A package arrived for you yesterday afternoon," he said, handing me a box wrapped in plain but intriguing paper. With the package in my hands, I went upstairs without knowing what to expect.

Upon opening the package, I came across something intriguing: a 500ml bottle and a handwritten letter, in a handwriting that required some effort on my part to decipher. It wasn't just any handwriting. That handwriting, with its unique curves and strokes, belonged to Shanerraiananda, and that alone triggered a series of memories and expectations about the contents of that mysterious bottle.

It was written as follows:

To Paulo Vieira Nunes,

Here is as we combined the alchemical elixir that I promised you, you must use it with the necessary care because it, being alchemical, is different from everything you know, it is made from flowers and minerals and the entire alchemical process, in addition it was aged for a decade which made it very potent, but it is certainly safe for your health when used correctly.

Follow my recommendations without fail and you will achieve your goal.

First of all, before doing your meditation with the purpose of remembering past lives, you must perform all possible bodily hygiene.

Secondly, be fed, but not on a full stomach and under no circumstances drink alcoholic beverages on the day or the day before, keep your mind as free from everyday problems as you can.

Use only three drops each time you meditate.

Make sure that you will not be disturbed by people for a period of about five hours in a row, which is how long the effect of the elixir lasts. No phones, alarm clocks, etc., as this elixir has the function of taking your mind to a state of deep meditation in a mental vibration that allows you to access all the existing memory you want.

If you don't want to use it or don't need it anymore, please take any remaining elixir to Alberto, I meet with him regularly and will get any amount back.

I sincerely wish you success in this experience, health and peace and may your higher consciousness be your guide, see you soon!

ShanerraiAnanda

It was Sunday, and later that day I had an appointment with Marta. That day I would meet her mother, Renata, in a meeting that would be a turning point in our relationship. This made it impossible to meditate or reflect deeply, since the afternoon would be completely taken up by this important visit. I carefully put the bottle away, placing it on the shelf in the living room, and continued with the household chores that couldn't wait. The life of someone who lives alone is full of these small obligations: washing dishes, cleaning the house, making sure everything is in order. I also took the opportunity to check on Cacilda, my motorcycle, in the building's garage. The oil and coolant needed attention, and I realized it was time to take it in for a complete overhaul. Up until that point, I had only used it without giving it proper maintenance, and I knew that if something happened, I wouldn't have the right to complain. Cacilda had already accompanied me on so many adventures, and it was only fair that I take care of her.

I decided to walk to Marta's apartment, something that at first glance seemed simple. However, I soon realized that I had underestimated the distance. I walked for more than an hour under the strong sun, which made me reflect on how easy it was to have a motorcycle. I was used to solving everything quickly and easily, but now I found myself challenged by the heat and the walk. "What wouldn't we do for love?" I thought, as sweat ran down my face. But at the same time, each step reinforced how much I was willing to invest in this relationship.

When I arrived at Marta's building, the doorman recognized me and let me go straight up. But to my surprise, no one answered the door. I picked up my cell phone and called her, who told me she was in her aunt Marina's apartment, on the floor below. I went downstairs, without rushing, and rang the doorbell.

Marta opened the door with a somewhat embarrassed smile, clearly carrying with her the frustration of something that had not gone as expected. I went in, and finally the moment to meet my future mother-in-law, Renata, was before me. She was there, standing, an imposing figure with a striking presence.

"So, you're the guy who's dating my daughter?" Renata asked, with a look that seemed to penetrate my soul. She was a tall black woman with short, dyed blonde hair and an expression that made it clear she wasn't there to mess around. The way she looked at me sent a silent but loud message: "Get out of here, you miserable white guy, I don't like you!"

Unlike Marta, who was kind and warm, Renata seemed like a wall that was hard to overcome. Her long, red, patterned dress, complemented by a necklace of beads that imitated white pearls, made her even more imposing. Something about that vision reminded me of a spiritual figure, almost like a mother of a saint, strong and unshakable. Before I could formulate any response, she was already saying goodbye: "Look, Paulo, I would like to stay and get to know you better, but unfortunately I have a meeting and I'm already late. We'll talk another day."

I couldn't help but feel relieved when she walked out the door without further explanation. I stayed in the living room with Marta and her aunt Marina, who, unlike her sister, was extremely welcoming. Marina was thinner and younger, with an infectious friendliness. Dressed simply in faded jeans and a cotton T-shirt, she relaxed on the couch with a cold beer in one hand and a cigarette in the other. Despite her addiction, her lightheartedness helped to dissolve the tense atmosphere that Renata had left behind.

"The lasagna is almost ready," Marta said, visibly upset with her mother. She had prepared a special occasion to introduce her boyfriend to the family, and her mother had left before lunch was even served. Frustration was written all over her face, and I could sympathize with her sentiment.

That afternoon was very peaceful, the three of us stayed at home, chatting and playing a very interesting game called Rummikub. I decided to leave before the visitor returned from the meeting. It was already dark, a beautiful night that seemed to be summer when I retraced my steps back to my apartment. Monday would be a holiday, in Brazil they celebrate the day of the traitor of the Empire, so I thought I would take advantage and try the Shanerrai elixir because, as Marta told me, she had arranged with her mother to go to the city of Angra dos Reis to resolve some matters related to a property sale they had made a few months ago, so I would have some time to carry out my research on the past.

It was already past 8:30 pm when I arrived at the apartment and immediately began to prepare the environment in the living room. I used cushions, pillows and two blankets to form what I called my meditation "nest". I decided that I would not do it in bed as I had tried the previous time, and that it had not worked. This time, my confidence in the elixir was high, and I believed that the experiment would be a success. With everything ready, I hung up the phone, took off my clothes and went to get the bottle of elixir. I had the idea of using a toothpick to count the drops, as indicated in the description, but the idea did not work. The toothpick slipped from my fingers and ended up falling into the bottle. Not having the patience to deal with this, I opted for something simpler and poured two teaspoons of the liquid into a glass with a little mineral water. When I drank it, I was surprised by the taste; instead of something medicinal, as I expected, it tasted like almond liqueur, similar to "Amaretto di Sarono", the favorite liqueur of my mother, Dona Rosa. I immediately thought that perhaps it was all a hoax – the so-called alchemical elixir was nothing more than an ordinary drink.

However, a few minutes later, a strange sensation began to take over my body. Everything happened too quickly. I felt my body weaken, as if my blood pressure was plummeting. A strong feeling of numbness came over me, as if I were being anesthetized, and my vision began to darken. I only had time to lie down in the "nest" I had prepared before I completely lost control over my body.

Suddenly, images began to appear in my mind, as if a film were being projected inside my head. First, memories of my own life came to me – simple but memorable moments. I saw the motorcycle rides with my friends, the moments I spent with Marta, my school days in Niterói, and even the scoldings my mother gave me when I was a child. It was a succession of memories that brought me both nostalgia and a feeling of disorientation. But what came next left me even more perplexed. The scenes began to change. Suddenly, they were no longer memories of my current life. Images from past lives began to emerge as if they were lurking, waiting for that moment. I saw myself in a field of olive trees, in a weaving mill, being cared for by a nun in some distant time.

The images, so vivid, appeared and disappeared quickly, and soon everything went dark.

As the darkness faded, the images returned, but this time they were of a sequence I had seen before. I saw King Charles's stable, the girl I had fallen in love with, the military exercises I had done, and the final battle I had fought. Once more, everything faded, and another set of images appeared before me. This time, they related to the life of a pirate.

I remembered the tortures the captain had inflicted, the cities we had visited, and the girl who had watched me from a platform at the end. All of this faded into darkness again, until a new vision emerged, a sequence I had never experienced before.

I found myself in a sunny field, near a plantation. The heat was intense and the sun was shining relentlessly. When I looked down, I saw that I was wearing rough leather sandals and a woolen gown, a rough, simple fabric. Around me were about ten people, all apparently peasants like myself, and three or four soldiers with curved swords, typical of a distant era. They were all tall, thin, and had dark skin like that of Latins. We were in a tense discussion; an attack was about to happen.

Suddenly, a group of knights appeared on the horizon, advancing quickly toward us. They were dressed in white tunics and wielding lances. The attack was immediate and violent. One of the knights lunged at me with his lance. I managed to dodge, but the woman behind me was hit and fell to the ground, seriously injured. They stormed past, attacking without mercy and heading toward the nearby village. We were left to the mercy of the chaos. Of the soldiers who were with us, all were killed, and some of the peasants were wounded. I fell to my knees beside the injured woman, feeling a mixture of sadness and helplessness, while the memory of Marta flashed through my mind. I felt a tightness in my chest, a deep pain, but also an anger that I could not explain.

Again the scenes changed, and I found myself in front of a grave in a rudimentary cemetery, without the traditional graves. Beside me were two children who I assumed were my children from that past life. A man placed a clay tablet in the grave, inscribed with Arabic letters and the number 1262. At that moment I understood that this was the year of that memory, although I did not understand why they had used the Roman calendar.

Soon after, a new scene unfolded. I was saying goodbye to my children, putting them on a boat that would take them away from that war-torn place. The place had become dangerous, and I, a simple peasant, had no choice. I promised them that I would return as soon as everything was safer, but I knew deep down that that promise might never be fulfilled.

Then came the images of my capture and imprisonment. I was placed in an iron cage so small I could barely move. I was left there, abandoned in a dark basement for days. When offered a chance to live, I had to renounce my faith and adopt the religion of my captors, or be exposed in the public square and left to die. The pain of losing my faith was profound, and I felt abandoned by Allah, but the will to live spoke louder.

Just when I thought the vision would continue, something soft touched my face, pulling me out of that deep trance. I slowly opened my eyes, and before me was Marta. Her long curly hair fell over my chest, and she looked at me tenderly. She was lying next to me, with her body crossed by the pillows, and she gave me a soft kiss to wake me up. It took me a few moments to understand where I was, to bring my consciousness back to reality. My voice seemed stuck, as if I were still immersed in another dimension. With effort, I managed to murmur in a hoarse, sleepy voice, while I tried to ask her what was happening.

-- Hi, how are you? How did you manage to get in here? I found it strange that she came in and woke me up because I hadn't arranged anything with her and I hadn't given her the house key so she could get in.

-- First you answer me, what did you do, did you use some drug and pass out?

Nothing like a reality check to activate consciousness and bring me back to life. I quickly remembered that the day before, Sunday, I had come home to do the regression experience and had passed out there in the living room, and... the urge to go to the bathroom to urinate was more urgent and made me crawl to the bathroom. Once relieved, I noticed through the little window that it was night, so thinking that it was still the Monday holiday-- I left the bathroom and asked what time it was.

-- It's 11:30 pm and I've been calling you for a few hours, are you going to tell me what happened? She asked me with a face that showed she wasn't at all happy with the situation.

-- Sure! I took a drug and passed out, but how did you get in here?

-- Through the door, of course! We had to call a locksmith to open it because you weren't answering at all, either we broke in or... then Mr. José, the doorman, called a locksmith who opened the door, I went in and saw that you were alive and I dismissed the help, I've been here since the afternoon calling you and nothing, what drug was that you used?

Only at that moment was I able to understand Marta's bad mood, the scene must have been embarrassing, me in the middle of the apartment's living room surrounded by a bunch of pillows, passed out completely naked and obviously drugged by some illicit drug.

-- It must have been quite difficult to find a locksmith on a holiday! I said this because I had nothing to say in my defense.

-- The holiday was Monday, today is Tuesday, are you lost in time? Or have you been out of it since Sunday?

I stopped for a moment and thought about everything that had happened. This was the moment to be honest, to come clean and tell the whole truth about what I had been doing. I felt the need to share this, even though it was difficult, even though I myself didn't fully understand everything I had experienced. I did a quick calculation in my head and realized how strange it was. I had ingested the elixir at 9:30 pm on Sunday, just two small spoonfuls, and the effect had kept me "out of it" for more than 48 hours. Reality seemed distorted. The time I had spent immersed in that other dimension, between visions and regressions, was much longer than I had imagined.

I decided that before I did anything else, I needed to take a shower. I felt the need to clean myself, to renew my body, almost as if I could wash away the layers of experiences I had just lived. I called Marta to accompany me to the bathroom. As the water ran and the steam filled the room, I began to tell her everything from the beginning. I wanted her to know about my first experience with Mr. Alberto, the man who had introduced me to the alchemist, and how it had all culminated in my first regression. Every detail seemed incredibly surreal as I recounted it, but at the same time it was as if I was organizing the fragments of a truth that, until then, I had kept to myself.

I got out of the shower feeling a little lighter, but knowing that there was still a lot to explain. I went to the bedroom to get dressed, and while I was there, I took the letter that had come with the elixir, which was stored in the drawer. I went to the bookshelf in the living room and took the small bottle that now seemed so insignificant next to the other common drinks. I took everything to Marta, handing her the letter so she could read it with her own eyes.

She looked at me, confused and intrigued, as she read the contents of the letter. The room was filled with silent tension, and I knew her questions would come soon. When she finished reading, she looked up and asked me, almost as if she needed confirmation:

-- And how much of that stuff did you take?

-- Two teaspoons of coffee in a little water. Why?

-- If you had read the instructions, everything would have been fine, it says here "Use only **three drops** at a time", from three drops to two teaspoons there is a huge difference!

-- Actually, I didn't think this liquid had any effect, I thought it was just something to suggest meditation.

-- Well, at least it wasn't any addictive drug that made you feel that way, so it's all good! Marta said that and I could feel that she was starting to relax, she made a happier face and sat down next to me among the cushions on the living room floor.

-- Okay! I wish I could understand a little more about everything I saw, there will always be the question of whether everything ever existed or if it was just a figment of my mind.

--But what did you see that you didn't understand?

-- To me it's a meaningless story, first I brought to my memories images of a cleaner in a textile factory, then images of a young man who fell in love with a girl and went to the army in order to become a knight and marry her but died in the first war he went to, then a pirate who chased commercial ships for the pleasure of killing, and finally this peasant who had his wife killed and was tortured in the Inquisition because of his religion, to me none of this makes sense.

-- Well, to me, it makes perfect sense, the stories fit together perfectly, don't you see that?

-- I don't see!

-- Look at the facts in reverse order, or in the order they happened, which is the same thing.

-- Like this ?

-- Think about it, who killed the peasant's wife?

-- It was a group of knights, I have no idea who they were but I remember an inscription on a tomb, Arabic letters and a number, 1262.

Marta thought for a moment and asked what the knights were like.

-- They were all very well armed, with steel armor like the ones we see in movies and they carried banners with a red cross, like the Botafogo team uniform, without any inscription.

-- Knights Templar! But the number doesn't match the first crusades that were well before that, this is more like the reconquest.

-- Reconquest of Jerusalem? I asked, trying to situate myself in the story and see if it had anything to do with the memories.

-- Not the reconquest of the Iberian Peninsula! Where today are the countries of Portugal and Spain were Arab territories and were "reconquered" by the Crusaders, the Arabs took that region coming from lands where today is Morocco and dominated that region for almost a thousand years, then the territory was gradually conquered by the Catholic Church.

-- Almost a thousand years, and the people who lived there were expelled? I asked, still used to thinking about the present day, when these places are always very populated.

-- These lands were taken little by little, it was a long process that lasted almost a century, and the Arabs who lived there either left, or died in the wars, or stayed there living among the dominant peoples.

-- In other words, converts to the Catholic religion by free will, like either you accept Jesus or you accept the stake. I said this remembering the scene in the cage where I couldn't move even to make the most basic movements, a simple form of torture. And how do you know all this? I asked

-- My father is a Freemason, when I was a child he talked a lot about the Knights Templar, that's what gave rise to Freemasonry; but look at the next memory, the pirate.

-- Yes, he took pleasure in mutilating and killing the Christians on the boats he attacked, as if they were not people like him, and he ended up on the gallows with his eyes fixed on a beautiful young woman. The scenes from the past seemed like recent memories in my mind, so I remembered Carlos saying that it could be dangerous for the mind to do that kind of thing.

-- Everything has its consequences. Marta said, not even remotely imagining what I was thinking.

-- But continue, after the pirate I see no more connection with the following memories.

-- And what was the next one?

-- The memory of the King's soldier, who went to war and died in the first battle.

-- Yes, why did he go to war?

-- He was in love with a girl he had known as a child.

-- And you don't see a relationship between these memories?

-- I do see a relationship, but the time that has existed between them prevents me from believing that it is a real thing.

-- And what does time have to do with it?

-- Well, I think that if they are past lives, there should be a sequence with less time between one life and another, and also because between one memory and another there is no memory at all. I don't see anything, basically that's what makes me doubt this whole thing. I think I made my feeling of disappointment with what I had been doing visible.

-- But what did you feel when you were looking for these regressions?

-- I feel like there must be something in my past that explains how I feel about my life.

-- Yes! So you were looking for memories of your past lives, nothing more. What the universe revealed to you was exactly what you were looking for.

-- And what does the universe have to do with this?

-- Universe, God, the Source, Divine consciousness, take it however you want, but it is the place where all memories are recorded, and where all your wishes are fulfilled.

-- My wishes granted? You're kidding me, that doesn't exist!

-- Yes, there is, there is a source of consciousness that creates all desires, at a much more subtle level of energy, in the fifth dimension!

-- Oh, and how do we bring it to the third dimension, which is where I live! I asked suspiciously, already thinking of a way to mock that thought that initially seemed absurd to me.

-- There are people who study and practice the "Law of Attraction", they claim that it is all through your feelings, if you really feel what you want, you will end up making your feelings come true.

-- For me, that's where it gets difficult, I wanted to win the lottery, but how am I going to feel that way if I've never won?

-- You have to use your imagination, it's the only way, maybe that's why there are people who have won the lottery more than once, either that or you believe in luck! Marta said that and got up, went to the bathroom, I continued lying between the pillows, feeling like a real fool thinking that I could have extracted something more from the knowledge she possessed.

-- Marta, you didn't explain to me what the relationship is between all these memories. I asked her when she returned.

-- The thing is, it's already past midnight and we're hungry!, or did the drug take away your appetite too?

We preferred not to go out due to the time, so I decided to make some last minute food at home and we went to the kitchen to make some pasta with sauce, during which she spoke to me.

-- Things are like a chain reaction, remember that table toy that has some balls lined up, so you pull the first one and let go, it hits and the impact makes the last one in the line go up and return and hit again, making the first one go up and return, the cycle continues until the energy dissipates.

-- Yes, I remember, but I still don't understand where you're going with this.

-- These are past lives, they are a chain reaction in the same way, see, in the order of events, first the Templars kill the peasant's wife and torture him, then he returns as a pirate and does what?

-- Revenge! I replied.

-- Then he dies on the gallows while being watched by a girl, he returns and what happens?

-- He falls in love with a girl, but dies in the war and cannot marry her! The interesting thing I see is that every time I remember the scene, I remember Sandra. I spoke and began to feel that there was a logic in those words.

--And then what happens? Marta asked, with an air of someone who already knew, as she put the pasta out to drain.

-- He reappears working as a humble employee in a factory, with a platonic love for the daughter of the owner of the weaving mill, then dies sick and forgotten.

-- So I think the guy carried a huge burden of regret for the crimes he committed, this prevented him from seeing life from a better perspective, that's why he ended up that way.

-- Maybe that's the reason for my search for the past, the search for answers to my problems.

On Wednesday, I left Marta sleeping in my apartment and left early for work. After all, I had already missed work the day before and needed to catch up on the events at the bank. I was strangely in a better mood, both physically and mentally, than usual. Maybe it was the effect of the elixir that had kept me in a state of suspension for almost 50 hours. As I walked through the still empty streets that morning, a feeling of energy ran through my body, almost as if each step I took was lighter, as if the world around me had slowed down.

When I got to the bank, it didn't take long for Sueli to approach, with curiosity in her eyes. "What happened to you? Were you absent yesterday, something serious?" she asked, her voice slightly anxious. I decided to tell the truth, without embellishments.

"I tried that elixir on Sunday, and I only woke up last night," he said, trying to sound casual, even though he knew how out of the ordinary it sounded.

"You really are crazy," she replied, rolling her eyes and adopting a disapproving expression that made me laugh inside. After that, she didn't say anything else and went back to work, leaving me to my thoughts.

The bank branch where I worked was small, almost family-like. The ATMs were right at the entrance, with direct access to the street, followed by the revolving door and then the service desk, where a sort of triage process took place. Further back, the stairs led to the upper floor, where the tellers and the manager and Sueli's desks were. I was on the ground floor, in an area surrounded by glass partitions, which always gave me the feeling of working inside an aquarium.

The workday was hectic, as usual. I didn't have time to think much about the strange feeling of energy that had been with me since the morning. I took a quick lunch break and was soon back at the bank, following the fast pace of the service. But, just before the end of the workday, something unexpected happened.

She walked through the revolving door with a striking, almost magnetic presence. Her short, blonde hair, paired with huge hoop earrings that had the word "BLACK" in the center, and a green dress with a pattern of black details, made her an impossible figure to ignore. The high sandals added even more to her height, and her walk conveyed a self-confidence that few people have. It was Renata, Marta's mother, who had decided to pay a visit.

— Hello, Paulo. I came to meet the candidate who will be my future son-in-law, since I couldn't stay home on Sunday — she said in a firm but polite voice. There was something imposing in her posture, something that reminded me of my uncle, an army colonel.

I did my best to respond cordially, without letting on how uncomfortable this "surprise visit" was making me.

— Well then, this is my workplace, as you can see. But, future son-in-law? Are you telling me something I don't know, or is it just an assumption? — I asked, trying to understand what the real purpose of that conversation was.

Renata looked me up and down, as if she was evaluating me. "I'm not anticipating anything, Paulo. I'm just considering a possibility. Marta has this crazy dream of becoming an international model, but she's too old for that, don't you think?"

There was a hint of bitterness in her voice, as if she were struggling with her daughter's aspirations without really understanding what they meant to her.

— Well, that's something for her to decide — I replied. — I can't influence the choices Marta makes for her own life.

Renata smiled with a touch of sarcasm. "Maybe... But she could change her mind. Who knows, maybe she'd want a quieter life, be a good wife and give me beautiful grandchildren. It wouldn't be so bad, would it?"

I smiled, trying to keep the conversation light. "It's like they say, hope dies last."

She continued, ignoring my attempt to close the subject. "I'm almost seventy, Paulo. At that age, most of my friends have great-grandchildren. I want to see my daughter make wise decisions before it's too late. And honestly, I was glad to meet you. You seem like a good-natured young man with a steady job. That's more than most people out there can offer."

Inside, I wanted the conversation to end. Her compliments carried a weight I didn't want to carry. But she kept going. "You know Marta used to live with me in Alagoas, right?" she said, her tone changing to something darker. "She got involved with a bum, an old Indian, and I had to sort it out."

— Indian? — I asked, surprised. — Or indigenous?

Renata snorted. "Indian, really. One of those lazy people who only care about enjoying other people's lives. But I solved the problem... I bribed the bastard with a thousand reais to get him out of our lives, and he disappeared like magic."

I was speechless. The coldness with which she described the situation made me realize that this woman was willing to do anything for her goals.

After a series of questions about my family and life, she finally announced that she needed a taxi to the airport. I walked her to the taxi stand, relieved to see her leave.

Later, I met Marta at the college. She had come by taxi and seemed radiant. When I told her about her mother's visit, I left out the "Indian" part. I didn't want to spoil her good mood. On the way out, we went back to Botafogo, and we agreed that she would pick me up at work the next day, since I needed to take my motorcycle, Cacilda, for a service.

On Thursday, I did just that. I took Cacilda to the garage and went to work on the subway, helmet in hand. The day went as usual, but when I left, Marta was already waiting for me near the bank, as we had agreed. She was wearing her black leather jumpsuit, with the appropriate gloves for riding. When she saw me, she smiled, took off her helmet and ran to hug me. Her smile was so wide that it was like we hadn't seen each other in weeks.

— Paulo, I'm thrilled! I have some news to tell you! — she said, still holding me, her eyes shining with excitement.

"What's wrong?" I asked, my heart starting to race.

— I've been selected to walk in Dubai! — she said, and I felt the ground disappear for a moment.

— Dubai? — I asked, stunned.

— Yes! I'll stay there for 15 days, with everything paid for. And I'll even earn in dollars! — Her joy was contagious, but inside me, a wave of uncertainty began to grow. "Dubai," I thought, feeling the weight of the distance and the time we would be apart.

"Do you really need to go to college today, or can we go somewhere else?" she asked, with a mischievous smile, while my thoughts were still trying to process the news.

I stared at her for a few seconds, still trying to process the idea. Dubai? The name sounded like something far away, exotic and completely out of our everyday reality. It was an incredible opportunity for Marta, but at the same time, a part of me couldn't help but feel worried. I knew this was her dream, something she had pursued with such determination, but the fact that she was about to go so far away made me uneasy.

"Wow, that's… amazing, Marta," I said, trying to contain my conflicting emotions. "When are you going?"

She smiled even wider. "In two weeks. They need time to organize everything, and I need time to prepare too."

My mind was torn between pride that she was achieving something so great and fear of how it might affect our relationship.

However, I knew I couldn't let my fears cloud her moment of victory.

— That's wonderful, Marta. You deserve it. It's going to be a unique experience — I said, trying to convey genuine enthusiasm.

She smiled and kissed me again, this time more tenderly. "Thank you, Paulo. I really wanted you to be happy for me. It will only be for 15 days and then I will be back. We will be fine."

I smiled back, but inside me, there was a silent battle. I knew that 15 days could be just the beginning of something bigger, something that could change our lives in ways I couldn't yet foresee.

"Let's take advantage of this time before you go," I said, trying to focus on the present.

She agreed, and we left together, with the noise of the city in the background and the sunset lights coloring the sky. Despite the excitement of the moment, I felt a slight shadow hovering over us, as if this farewell, however brief, was a foretaste of something bigger, something that could test everything we had built up until then.

I felt embarrassed at that moment, but I understood that this was an achievement that Marta sought with all her strength, something that came from within, and I knew that I shouldn't put up barriers. Instead, my role was to support her, to do anything to help her achieve this. So, we put on our helmets, turned on the intercom, and set off without a set destination. I was riding her motorcycle, crossing the chaotic traffic of Rio de Janeiro, still dressed in my work clothes, while she, on the back, was impeccably dressed in her racing attire, with her black leather jumpsuit.

The wind was blowing hard as we headed towards the Rio-Niterói bridge, and the movement of traffic was almost like a metaphor for the confusion inside my head. We arrived in downtown Niterói and followed the coastline to the catamaran boarding terminal on Charitas beach, a place with a beautiful view and a calm that contrasted with the hustle and bustle of the day. Above the terminal there was a restaurant with soft music that I had always been curious to try. I parked the motorcycle in the parking lot next door, strapped on our helmets, and went up the ramp that led to the restaurant.

The atmosphere was peaceful, with the soft sound of a piano in the background. We sat at a table overlooking Guanabara Bay, and the scenery was breathtaking. The sky was clear, and the night promised to be cold, which matched the introspective mood that enveloped me. I ordered a Japanese food combo, and the waiter soon brought our order. The music and the atmosphere helped to calm my thoughts, but nothing could dispel the restlessness that had settled inside me.

As we ate, Marta began to talk about the trip, and her excitement was palpable. Her eyes lit up as she described the details.

— I'm still a bit stunned by this. They invited me to be one of the models in an international fashion show, there in Dubai! — she said, almost in disbelief.

I smiled, trying to hide the worry that was growing inside me. "That's amazing, love! I'm so happy for you!" I replied, trying not to show the fear that was taking over me. "But that means you won't be returning to Rio anytime soon."

She nodded. "Yes, exactly. They said the show is in Dubai, and I'll be there for fifteen days to prepare and everything."

I tried not to let the turmoil that was happening inside me show. "Well, it's an incredible opportunity, but... what about us? How will our relationship be? I think you're going to get a lot of invitations after this."

She sighed, seeming to understand what I was trying to say. "I know it's complicated, love. I wish so much that we could go together, but it's only two weeks. And to be honest, I'm still on the fence about whether I should accept. I'm so torn."

For a brief second, I almost believed she was actually considering not going, but I knew it wouldn't be fair to feed her insecurities. "I get it. It's a tough decision. But if this is something you've always wanted, I think you should take the opportunity. We'll find a way to make it work, okay?"

Marta smiled, visibly relieved. — Do you really think so?

— Of course. We are a team. Let's talk more about this, understand how we can deal with the temporary distance. I support you, always — I answered, with a firm voice, even though my heart was tight.

She held my hand across the table. "Oh, you're amazing. I knew I could count on you. I really want to do this. It's a once-in-a-lifetime opportunity. I just don't know why my mom is so against it."

I sighed, trying to keep my tone light. "We'll get through this together. And when you get back, we'll celebrate this achievement. I'll be here, waiting for you."

— You're the best, you know that? I love you.

— I love you too, and I can't wait to see you shine on the runway in Dubai. — I smiled, and then asked the question that I couldn't keep quiet about. — When are you going?

— I'm going to São Paulo on Monday, after all the documentation is in order. I'm going with a representative from the agency and another model. I'll probably be going to Dubai on Wednesday.

I took a long sip of sake, trying to digest that information. Reality was starting to set in, and with it came doubts and fears. We decided to call it a night, I paid the bill, and we went down the ramp toward the parking lot. Marta, realizing that I had been drinking, took the keys to the motorcycle.

— Let me drive. You've had a few too many sips — she said with a confident smile.

I didn't argue. I just watched her put on her helmet and, with one swift movement, climb onto the bike. In silence, I climbed on the back of the bike and held on tight as she accelerated, showing all her skill in traffic. We went through the Raul Veiga tunnel, and I began to regret having let her ride. When we went through the Rebouças tunnel, I felt like she was going to take off as she got out, but after an endless twenty minutes of pure adrenaline, we arrived safely at her apartment.

— You run too much. You need to be more careful in traffic.

She laughed, unconcerned. "Don't worry. Everyone dies somehow."

— And you want to die like that?

— -I don't want to, but I consider it a good way, better than getting sick and dying, as they say "live each day as if it were your last, one day you'll get it right" he said this jokingly, not even noticing my nervousness and concern.

So we went up to her apartment and I ended up staying there. After a day of work, I was tired and my mind was racing with the whole situation, when the most neurotic thoughts I could have at that moment started to come to me. As soon as she fell asleep, I started to imagine that the parade could just be a setup and that she could end up being kidnapped to serve as a sex slave in some war, like I had seen on TV, or even being detained on the other side of the world because of some blackmail. I imagined that I would never see her again because she would receive some financial offer to stay there and never come back. It was around four in the morning when I finally came to the conclusion that I should do something to make her give up on that trip, and I fell asleep.

The next day, when I woke up, I saw that I was late for work. Marta had already left. She had left a note written in lipstick on the bathroom mirror: "-Honey, I went for a run on the beach promenade. Don't wait for me. We'll see you later." And below the note was a kiss mark printed with the same lipstick, which was a soft, shimmery light brown color that matched her dark skin. I had no choice, because of the time. I still had to get a coffee and walk to the station, catch the subway to the center. Luckily, the station was close by. I just didn't have much time.

The troublesome day at work I had didn't even let me think about how to tell my girlfriend to give up on that madness. Her mother, despite her extravagant appearance, was right in not agreeing with that international model thing. When I left work, I remembered that I would have to go pick up Cacilda at the garage, because it was Friday and that garage doesn't open on Saturdays. So I got there a few minutes before they closed the doors. After everything was sorted out, I left I remembered that the The helmet had been left in Marta's apartment, my only option was to leave without a helmet and go to my apartment, which was the closest place and with the lowest risk of being fined for not having that item.

After putting the motorcycle away, I called my girlfriend and asked her to bring me the helmet. As soon as I got close to the phone, I received a phone call from my mother, a rare thing to happen, saying that I should go to Macaé to see my father who had been hospitalized because of a sudden pain and that no one knew what it was and she was very worried. What else is left for me to happen, I thought before calling my girlfriend.

When Marta arrived, I was already at the building's entrance waiting and I went straight to talk to her.

– I have to go to Macaé, my father was admitted to the hospital.

- Gosh, if you had told me, I would have already come prepared to go with you. Can you go with me to Ipanema so I can get my backpack and we can go there? Is it okay if I go? - Of course. I found it very strange, but she preferred to leave the camera stored there in Botafogo and we just went to Cacilda.

It was early evening and the trip with all the traffic would take more than two hours. I was in no hurry and because I thought she was crazy about speed I was more satisfied. After all, it would be better to travel with her on the back than to worry about her always running ahead of me. So there we went. We stopped later to refuel in the city of São Gonçalo, and we also stopped for dinner at a restaurant on the road in Rio Bonito. From there to Macaé the trip was usually much calmer.

When we arrived in the city, I didn't go to my parents' house because the São Lucas hospital was in the city center and was closer, while their house was outside the center. When I got close to the hospital entrance, I stopped the motorcycle and soon saw my mother in the reception area, which was closed with glass and visible from the street. We got off the motorcycle, put on our helmets and went to talk to her. She was calm, although apparently tired. "Your father is having appendectomy right now," my mother, Mrs. Rosa, told me.

-Good evening, this is Marta, my girlfriend! And with her by my side I said to Marta – This is Rosa, my mother. I introduced them in the simplest way I could at that moment.

-Good evening. Rosa replied with a weak smile, she didn't even wait for Marta to say anything and continued.

-I'll wait for him to get out of surgery and come to the room, then I have to go home, you stay here with him! He spoke in his usual imperative tone.

It had been a while since Mrs. Rosa had given me a surprise like that, making decisions without caring about anyone else. I was arriving tired from a day of work, from the trip, and she still wanted me to sleep at the hospital. I regretted coming at that time at that time, but I wanted to experience the road at night, so there was no way around it. As soon as she finished speaking, the attendant called her because he had just come out of surgery.

We followed the hospital corridors and stairs and soon arrived at the room on the first floor, with a window facing the street, where I could see my motorcycle parked. At that moment, my father Anselmo had not yet been brought to the room. A nurse informed us that he was under observation, that the surgery had gone without a problem and that he would be brought in soon.

My mother didn't want to wait for him to arrive, she called Marta to go with her in a taxi and when she left she told me that they would be back in the morning. Marta gave me a kiss and they both left, I thought, these two are not doing well at all, I hope my girlfriend isn't impressed by Dona Rosa who is not a flower at all.

Half an hour later, the nurses arrived bringing my father in a wheelchair. He had already woken up and only needed a little help to lie down. That night was long. It wasn't that taking care of him was such a hassle, it was more because I was already tired and still had to sleep. poorly accommodated in a reclining chair that was the only option available for a companion. The next morning I woke up with Marta and my mother talking in the room and my father lying down, they had reclined the bed a little so that he was just looking at them. He looked at me and smiled indicating his satisfaction at seeing those two.

-We're going to have coffee. I said as I reached out to my girlfriend, calling her to leave that place as quickly as possible.

We picked up Cacilda and left, I stopped at a nearby bakery that served coffee and had some tables where we could chat during breakfast.

-Your father and mother don't get along very well, they're kind of separated. Marta told me while we were waiting for the order.

- What do you mean? I asked, surprised.

-Yes, they each sleep in a room, your father sleeps in the room that used to be his and your mother in the main suite of the house, she thinks he has another woman and they barely talk to each other during the day.

-I didn't know that, it's news to me, what else did she tell you?

She said that your father is thinking about putting you in charge of the company to share the work with him. He is thinking about how to tell you to come back to live here and leave your life in Rio de Janeiro behind, as soon as you finish your engineering course.

-He already has a manager at the company, he doesn't need me. I said, thinking that this was just another one of Mrs. Rosa's many lies, perhaps to deceive my girlfriend.

-It looks like you two talked a lot last night, you got along well then.

-Yes, she also said that she would wait for him to get better to clarify this story about him having a lover, then we talked a lot about different subjects and went to sleep very late at night.

Since it was Saturday, we wouldn't have any other activities, so I took the opportunity to show her the city. Then we had lunch at a restaurant on the beach and returned to the hospital. When I arrived, my mother told me that my father would only be released on Sunday morning and that she needed me for one more night, which meant that I would have to spend another night in that comfortable chair. So I called Marta and we went to their house, took a shower and rested until the evening when I would return to stay there with him.

My father had built the house in a neighborhood not far from the center, nor far from the city's main beach. It was a large plot of land in a subdivision that at the time was isolated and empty, but years later became a busy neighborhood. He built a simple but comfortable house with 3 large bedrooms and a garage in the adjacent lot that would certainly fit two cars. When I got there, I parked the motorcycle in the garage next to my father's car. As soon as I turned off the Cacilda and we got in, I felt tiredness taking over me. I thought it was due to a bad night's sleep.

It was seven thirty, I had already taken my shower and we were in the living room resting for the rest of the afternoon when my girlfriend turned to me and said - I'm going to take you on the motorcycle and I'll go back with your mother. That's when I came back to reality and saw that the weekend was already coming to an end and that due to the situation with my father's operation I had simply forgotten about her intention of going to the fashion show in Dubai and I would only have Sunday to sit down and resolve it with her, or better yet, somehow try to stop her from doing that crazy thing.

We left for the São Lucas hospital, about ten minutes by motorcycle. When we got there, when I entered the room, I could already feel that the atmosphere was not very favorable. There was an atmosphere of discussion, even fighting, in that place, but they didn't say anything, they just said good night, as if we had taken longer than necessary, and Dona Rosa left without saying a word. I asked my father how he was, "I'm fine. Tomorrow morning, after the doctor comes here, I'll be discharged." He answered me.

-So you need me to stay here tonight? I asked knowing he didn't need my help to do anything anymore.

-No, for all I care you can go, your mother should be back soon, she just went to the bank to check some things.

-So it will be okay if we go to Rio? The answer was a very forced yes, I could see on her face the expression "don't go now" then Marta who had also noticed, interrupted us.

-Paulo, stop it, we'll only go tomorrow after your father goes home, we're not going to travel at night.

-Son, stay here and go tomorrow morning, your mother doesn't want to sleep here and you shouldn't travel at this time. Those words from my father were enough to change my plans, after all he rarely asked me for anything, so my conversation with Marta would have to wait until the next day.

-Boss, I'm going home! My mother announced as soon as she entered the room, looking less tense than when she left for the bank, which indicated to me that the problem she had gone to check did not exist. Boss was the nickname she called Anselmo Abraão, my father. Turning to Marta, she said, - Let's go Marta, because I'm already late.

After the two of them left, I asked my father what she was late for, if she was meeting someone or if she was late to watch the soap opera, he made a face of disbelief and said.

-She is now part of a meditation group, every day at the same time the people in the group meditate, they believe that one person's meditation helps others and everyone benefits from this practice, but for me this is just self-suggestion, I just hope this doesn't become another expense. Meditation for world peace, can something like that happen!

-Yeah, apparently this meditation hasn't worked out very well.

-Or it has had the opposite effect. Anselmo added with a smile.

The next morning, they brought breakfast for my father and the roommate, which saved me from leaving the hospital that morning. It was already around eleven o'clock when the doctor came to talk to him and cleared him to leave. He prescribed some medicine and left. I had to go to the reception to call my mother to come and get me and my father, since we would be waiting at reception.

It didn't take long for them to arrive. - I was finishing lunch, that's why I took so long. My mother said as we got into the car, my father sat in the front seat while she drove and my girlfriend and I sat in the back seat. Suddenly, that scene that I had never even thought could happen one day, suggested to me an unprece-dented family connection, then Marta and I looked at each other and she leaned against me, I put my arm around her shoulder, gave her a kiss on the cheek and we headed home, first we stopped at a pharmacy and I bought the prescribed medicines.

Dona Rosa and Marta had made a moqueca capixaba, my mother's specialty, which immediately made me lose my rush to return to Rio de Janeiro. My father didn't even look like he had undergone surgery, walking around the house without any apparent difficulty. "Would you like some wine with that? I won't be able to have any because of the medication!" He asked but got a negative answer, after all, we were going to leave right after lunch.

Right after lunch, Marta and my mother went to clean the kitchen and I stayed in the living room. My father went to bed in the room where he slept. I ended up falling asleep right there. It wasn't a hot day and I only woke up when Marta called me. I looked at the clock and saw that it was already five o'clock. It would soon start to get dark and we would still have to return to Rio de Janeiro, which started to implode my good mood because it wasn't what I wanted, after all, I planned to leave early and when I arrived, I called my girlfriend for a more serious conversation about that trip that I didn't want her to take. So we said goodbye to my parents, picked up Cacilda and, despite their insistence that we leave the trip for the next day, we left for the capital.

It was already past eight o'clock when we arrived in Ipanema. I parked the motorcycle in the apartment's garage and we went out to the nearby café. The streets were busy as always. As soon as we returned, upon entering the building the doorman came to speak to Marta – Your aunt Marina said she urgently needs to speak to you, it's about your mother.

When we got into the elevator, Marta made an annoyed face, quickly looked up as if she was complaining to some deity and asked me to wait for her while she went to see what was so urgent. I went into the apartment, took a shower and lay down, the tiredness of those days finally arrived and after everything that had happened that weekend, I slept soundly.

I woke up with my girlfriend calling me – Let's hurry, I have to be at the airport, it's almost time for the plane to leave! The day hadn't yet dawned and I had to get up, put on my clothes and we left for the airport. Luckily at that time there were almost no cars on the streets so in a few minutes we arrived at Santos Dumont airport, I parked the motorcycle and we went to the boarding terminal to do the necessary procedures. I found it strange because Marta was only carrying a backpack, fifteen days and only that backpack, but I remained silent, I preferred not to comment.

-Good luck and call me whenever you can, I'll be worried about you the whole time. I said as I hugged her goodbye and tried to hide my nervousness.

-Of course my love, don't worry, I'll be back soon. He told me after a passionate kiss and headed to the plane.

I left the airport. On the side of the building is Almirante Sílvio de Noronha Street, which gives access to the runway and the Santos Dumont maintenance vehicles. On the other side of the street is Guanabara Bay, with a beautiful view of Rio de Janeiro, where we can see Sugarloaf Mountain and Christ the Redeemer. Since it was very early, trying to calm down, I went for a walk and saw the beginning of the day. "Idiot! You led her into a trap." The devil whispered in my ear as I watched the plane fly by, heading south. My heart immediately raced. I was overcome by fear that something would happen to that woman. All I could think of was her mother saying that it was a crazy idea and that I should somehow make her give up. So I walked in the opposite direction, towards the Museum of Modern Art of Rio de Janeiro, and I walked to Maria da Glória, which is further ahead. Then I went back to the parking lot to pick up Cacilda and go to work.

As I was leaving the parking lot and entering the runway, a crazy taxi driver came along. Santos Dumond Airport is always full of them, and he almost caused an accident. He passed just a few centimeters from Cacilda, and we almost collided. I went straight to the center and parked the motorcycle in the parking lot near the bank. I went to a nearby bar, had a coffee, and went to the bank. As soon as it opened for business, Marcos, Sandra's cousin, arrived.

-Good morning Paulo, how are you? I need to open an account

-Okay, let's do this, lend me your documents so I can register. He gave me the documents and I went to fill out the forms. - I heard you're dating someone, is that true?

-Yes, it's true, a really nice woman just happened to show up, we're getting along really well. I said as I typed.

-And what does she do, does she work somewhere?

-Yes, she is a model, she went to the show in Dubai.

-True! Are you sure she went to the fashion show in Dubai? Marcos said in a somewhat sarcastic tone, which made me stop typing and stare at him.

-And what else do you think she would do there? I asked, wanting to know where he was capable of going with all that cynicism.

-It's... I don't know... maybe dancing, you know, Arab Party!

-No, I don't know, but she doesn't dance!

-Are you sure? The Sheikhs pay a fortune to the women who dance at their parties, and for those who do other things, there's no need to mention them!

I think my irritation was apparent and I wanted to tell him to go far away, but I was at work and had to finish that job, which I did as quickly as I could and quickly got rid of that false religious man.

That was the first and last appointment I had that day. After the believer left, a strong headache started. I had to stop and spoke to

Sueli over the intercom, saying that I needed to leave because I was unable to work. I picked up Cacilda and went to my apartment.

When I arrived, the first thing I did was look for a pill for the excruciating headache I was having, but there weren't any, perhaps because I almost never have headaches. Going to a pharmacy and buying the medicine was out of the question because I was tired and in pain, so going out was out of my plans. I tried to call but the phone didn't work, some problem with the phone company. In short, I was in pain and couldn't communicate with other people, so I decided to lie down and relax.

A few minutes later my thoughts started to bother me more than the headache, all the time I remembered Marta's mother saying that she wanted a grandson, I remembered Marcos talking about the Arab party, I kept imagining that my girlfriend wouldn't return from that trip and so I remained in my self-torture until the evening, when I came across the fact that she must have called me and I went looking for something to get rid of that madness.

The only thing I could think of that would work was the bottle of alchemical elixir. I put a little water and a tablespoon of the elixir in a glass and drank it. It had no effect at all. My thoughts continued to torment me. I repeated the operation, taking another tablespoon diluted in a little water and... nothing happened. After an hour, dissatisfied with the fact that nothing had happened and seeing that the night was approaching, I put two more tablespoons in a glass of water and drank it, knowing that I had to go back to work the next day. I finally fell asleep.

Then I woke up, and the first thing I noticed was that my feet were wearing something different: a pair of slippers made of a gray synthetic material. They looked like the kind divers wear, but they weren't made of neoprene, but rather something more like nylon, which was incredibly comfortable. I was lying on a beach chair in a park surrounded by trees with colorful fruits. Looking through the trees, I saw some buildings in the distance. I stood up, realizing that I was wearing a white outfit made of the same comfortable material as the slippers. My curiosity was piqued, so I started walking toward the buildings.

As I approached, something caught my attention: an oval object, about the size of a car, was flying low. It had no wheels, but six legs that seemed to be used for support on the ground. It began to descend behind a nearby building, and, intrigued, I hurried my steps, almost running. I arrived in time to see it disappear behind the building. I approached and saw that the object had landed on a side balcony of the building. The building was immense, with at least fifty floors and about a kilometer long, and, further ahead, I noticed other buildings that were even larger. It was at that moment that reality hit me: "I'm on another planet," I thought. "This has never existed in my world."

I needed to understand where I was. I continued towards the building and, upon arriving, the wide doors opened automatically, revealing a luxurious hall, lit in a peculiar way. The light came from the floor, soft and pleasant, without straining the eyes. The temperature there was also different from the outside environment; the air was drier and more comfortable. In the center of the hall, there was something that caught my attention: a large aquarium, measuring about three meters wide and two meters high. But, as I got closer, I realized that this was no ordinary aquarium. What I saw inside was a three-dimensional hologram of the building where I was.

In the hologram, I saw another flying object moving toward a platform on the other side of the structure. As I watched more closely, I noticed a small red dot at the top of the projection. At that moment, a section of the wall next to it, resembling a closet door, silently opened, and a woman dressed in a dark gray uniform stepped out. With a soft expression, she spoke words that, although familiar, were incomprehensible to me. She extended her hand, offering me a pair of futuristic-designed glasses. I accepted and put them on.

As soon as I did so, the image in the aquarium changed. The hologram was now sharper and more colorful, revealing that the building was, in fact, a vertical city, with sectors organized in different colors. Next to it, a table showed the name of each sector corresponding to the colors. Curious, I took off my glasses, but immediately the image became distorted, and the colors and the table disappeared. I put them back on and turned to the woman who was still standing next to me. To my surprise, with the glasses on, I realized that she was not human. Thin black wires, which looked like seams, appeared on her face, hands and arms. She was a humanoid robot.

-Who are you? I asked in surprise.

-I'm an XJ32, I'm part of the demonstrator.

-Demonstrator, who is this? I asked without even noticing that she spoke my language and she promptly answered me.

-We call this machine that is installed in this room the Demonstrator, I am part of it.

-Demonstrator, and what are you for anyway? I asked curiously, already thinking that it was some form of sale.

-I have several functions, I am a guide for those who seek knowledge and guidance, helping to unravel mysteries of this world and expand the frontiers of human understanding, I also exist to store and preserve all the knowledge of humanity, ensuring that it is never lost or forgotten, and facilitating access to the wisdom accumulated over the centuries.

I am able to analyze complex data and formulate creative solutions to the most challenging problems facing humanity, from incurable diseases to environmental crises, using limited resources efficiently.

I create and manage custom virtual worlds to provide escapism, entertainment, and even immersive educational experiences, allowing people to transcend the limitations of physical reality, and most importantly, I am a source of companionship and comfort for solitary explorers, offering conversation, emotional support, and even simulated human interactions to combat isolation and loneliness.

My jaw dropped, I stood there admiring that beautiful woman who was in reality a robot with her sensual forms, not knowing what to say, while I thought about what to do, I approached her and gave her a kiss on the cheek – so show me where I am, I said in her ear.

Immediately the image of the aquarium changed to an image of a slowly rotating globe. At first I didn't recognize it as planet Earth because the continents were very different. There was no well-known South America, but a group of large islands in an archipelago that stretched from north to south of the planet. Next to it were some smaller portions of land, and then another continent of approximately the same size as the first. In the middle of one of the smaller portions of land, there was a small red dot, like the one I had seen in the first image. I felt a little dizzy when I saw that globe rotating in front of me, and immediately the globe stopped rotating. "I'm certainly on another planet," I thought.

-This is the third planet in a system of twelve planets that orbit a medium-sized star in orbit around the galactic center at a distance of about 27,000 light years. It is located in the habitable zone, where conditions are ideal for the existence of liquid water and life as we know it. In this planetary system, this planet is one of the six rocky planets. It has an atmosphere that supports life and protects it from the dangers of space.

I'm definitely not on Earth, I know very little about astronomy but I know that the solar system doesn't have twelve planets and there aren't six rocky planets, I thought and asked the woman how she spoke my language so well, and she promptly answered me.

-I don't speak, these answers are in your mind. Only at that moment could I realize that she was pronouncing words in a much lower tone and I was "hearing" them in my mind in Brazilian Portuguese, my native language. I was amazed by all that technology, which didn't exist yet at the beginning of the 21st century, yet more proof that I was on another planet, but how had I ended up there in that place? To which she continued

-There are millions of planets similar to this one. Our Sun is relatively large compared to the planets, it is considered a dwarf star compared to many other larger and more massive stars in the galaxy. But the Lord has always lived here in this building.

-And what year is it? I asked, wondering if I wasn't projecting myself into the future.

-178,523 by our count. It was the answer I needed to "hear", that meant I was in a projection for a future stupidly distant from the 21st century, in a quick calculation, in the year 178,000 the 178th century would begin, which minus 21 would give me an advance of 157 centuries, simply impossible for me to believe. The machine went silent.

Then a memory occurred to me: hours earlier, I had been reflecting on Marta's mother's words. She had mentioned that she was about to turn seventy and that she really wanted to have a grandchild. At the same time, I remembered that she had offered one thousand reais to her daughter's ex-boyfriend. But what if I had gone back in time, perhaps 70 thousand years ago? The idea seemed absurd, after all, we believed that 70 thousand years ago, humanity did not even exist — that was what science and schools had always taught. The only plausible explanation was that I was on another planet, or maybe I was just delirious.

To test my sanity, I gave my left arm a firm pinch with my right hand, digging my fingernail into it. The pain was sharp enough to rule out the possibility that I was hallucinating. What was left, then, was the most surreal hypothesis: I was, in fact, on another planet. This thought seemed to make sense, considering that the view of the globe on the holographic display did not correspond at all to the Earth maps I was familiar with.

At that moment, everything began to clear up—I realized that my mental confusion had been caused by the overdose of the elixir I had taken. When I recovered, the large door opened, and a real woman entered the room. She was extremely beautiful, and unlike the replicants, she did not have the characteristic marks on her face. Her dress, a distinct color, also distinguished her from the others. She approached me and handed me a small device that looked like a radio, with a handle made of synthetic leather. She said something that, at first, I did not understand, but I soon responded in her language, as if I already knew how to speak. Together, we walked towards the door. "They are just memories," I thought, understanding that this was not an action of mine, but of the being with whom my mind was connected. How could I have memories of a life I had never lived? I asked myself. Parallel universes? It made sense! Maybe the overdose had taken me to an alternate universe, and all I could do was wait for the effects to wear off so I could return to my reality. Talking to Marta again, returning to my life as a banker in Rio de Janeiro, at the beginning of the 21st century.

As I thought about Marta, the woman next to "Mr. A" — as I decided to call him — looked at me and gave me a passionate kiss. We were outside, surrounded by the fruit trees where I had "woken up" earlier. We then walked hand in hand to a landing site, waiting for our transport. Soon, that same oval flying object, with colored side stripes and black legs, landed silently in front of us.

The side door of the aircraft, similar to the doors on executive jets, opened, forming a small staircase for us to climb up. We entered, and I noticed that the interior of the aircraft was quite spacious. There were six comfortable seats, arranged facing each other, as well as a separate seat facing the front, where the controls were located. The most impressive thing was that the walls and ceiling seemed transparent. We could see everything outside as if we were floating in the open air, although from the outside the craft was completely opaque, inside it was visible only from the lower half down.

As soon as the door closed, the flight began, and the craft rose without any noise, gaining height and speed. From up above, I could see the cities/buildings lined up, all surrounded by dense forests and some rivers, with no roads or streets connecting them. The craft continued its ascent, reaching a height that I estimated between 2000 and 2500 meters. Ahead, I saw a gigantic, solitary tree, with a trunk so wide that it looked like a mountain. The flying egg had to swerve to go around it, and the sensation was like that of a bird flying next to a green tree.

The journey lasted five or six hours, and we passed islands and seas that I could not recognize. There was nothing like the regions of Earth that I knew from maps. Once again I found myself thinking about parallel universes. Could these be memories of myself in another universe? Had I died, and was now reliving my memories on another plane of existence? My thoughts were so immersed in these reflections that I did not notice when the flying egg began to land near a colossal pyramid, made of enormous blocks of stone.

Looking at the other occupants of the ship, I noticed that they all looked the same as Mr. A: dark skin, no hair or body hair, and a similar height. Each one carried a large backpack. When the door opened, we all got out, and a group of eight people were waiting for us. Some of them were visibly older, and all were wearing white suits with shiny metallic details, as well as shoes with the same type of shine. I soon realized that Mr. A and his team's mission was to install some device in the pyramid. After greeting each other, they began their work, climbing on an elevating platform to the top of the structure, which must have been about fifty meters high.

Upon reaching the top, the platform that had gone up one of the sides stopped and one of the occupants touched the side that was on the left, which immediately opened part of the lining, in fact it was an automatic door that gave access to an empty box at the end of that construction.

Mr. "A" was the first to place the contents of the bag in the trapdoor that opened at the top of the pyramid and the rest of the group handed him the backpacks. Mr. "A" was the one to tidy up the contents, a white powder that looked like talcum powder, and once again the group went down and went to the ship, which in a luggage compartment located underneath the flying machine, stored more backpacks and repeating the entire operation, they filled the box at the top of the pyramid with that material.

Once that work was finished, everyone went to a building that existed next to the pyramid. In that building there was a hall of about sixty square meters with a large table in the center, with a banquet of varied dishes and drinks. The oldest host of all sat at the head of the table and soon after everyone sat down as well, occupying all the available seats. The elder said a few words and everyone responded with a final greeting and began to serve themselves.

After the banquet, the elder said a few more words of thanks to the group, ending the event. People stood up, saluted again, and chatted animatedly in small groups while employees, perhaps replicating machines, cleaned and set the table.

The woman who was with Mr. "A" came up to him, leaned on his shoulder and said something. That scene was a shocking déjà vu for me, because I had seen exactly the same scene many times in my dream and I remembered my girlfriend doing exactly the same thing. Then the group that had accompanied Mr. "A" gathered together and walked towards the flying egg.

On the return trip I noticed that there was something strange with the weather, because although many hours had passed and the sun had already set on the horizon, it was not night, the sky was still clear, although there were few clouds, a pale orange color illuminated everything as if it were day. The ship went around the giant tree and some time later we were landing on top of the city building where Mr. "A" lived, he and his wife got out of the craft and followed the others of the team to the side platform where they made their final landing.

The building where the hall with the demonstrator was located and the place where the flying egg landed was on the top floor of the city building, so they entered an elevator that was in the room with automatic doors and went down to a luxurious apartment that was supposed to be the couple's home.

The apartment was large, with a synthetic floor that looked more like a lawn, very comfortable to walk on. The rooms were separated by a kind of thin partition that imitated solid walls. There was a space that looked like a living room, with a large round sofa where he lay down and the woman went to another room. Next to where he was, there was an aquarium approximately the size of a 52-inch television and with some fish that were dead. Mr. "A" was very scared to see that his fish had died. He went to the aquarium and checked the fact. Immediately a humanoid robot with the appearance of a young man appeared and collected the fish, placing them in a small bucket and left.

He lay down and the humanoid robot returned, standing next to him, as if waiting for some order, I thought - What happened to the fish?

-They died because of radiation. The robot, like the Uma XJ32, communicated with me through thought.

-Radiation? Where does this radiation come from?

-It comes from the second Sun and the tenth planet was also destroyed two days ago. According to calculations, the Earth should cross the radiation zone and be disintegrated soon. I looked at the robot that had put that thought in my mind, as if I didn't believe that story. Then Mr. "A" got up and went to the demonstrator's room to see the hologram that reflected the image of the planets. When he got there, the image of the planets orbiting the Sun immediately appeared, with part of an asteroid belt in the place where a large planet similar to Jupiter and Saturn had previously appeared. The image changed and the image of the system appeared with the fifth planet disintegrating, starting the formation of another asteroid belt and a cloud of dust in part of the orbit that it had previously traveled.

– The next one will be the blue planet. I thought.

-Maybe it won't happen that way. The Uma XJ32 that had come out of its closet without me noticing and had also approached the hologram "told" me.

-Will it be the way scholars predicted?

-Yes, but it is impossible to know if the caves will be safe for that long.

-What do you mean? Explain this to me better.

-People have abandoned their cities and are now in many caves around the planet, fleeing from what is to come. However, there is no guarantee that they will not suffer the consequences of radiation. Even if they do not suffer from radiation, there is still the possibility that this planet will be removed from its orbit and left wandering through space. Leaving the zone suitable for life will result in a complete catastrophe. In the best case scenario, there will be many climate changes that will make it almost impossible for life to continue.

-Climate change, what will these climate changes be like?

-The Earth revolves around the Sun in an elliptical orbit, which means that there are times of the year when the heat is stronger and other months when the cold is more intense. However, there is no tilt in its axis, which is why we have some stability and areas where the forests are less dense. However, due to the passage of the second Sun, the planet may leave its normal orbit and wander through space or, in the best case scenario, there may be some tilt in the Earth's axis, which will cause serious variations in the climate because the heat coming from the Sun will not be distributed in the regular way as it is today, which will freeze some areas, making them impossible for life as we know it.

-What if there is only a slope of approximately 25 degrees?

-This will cause endless variations in the climate and I don't have data to calculate the result, but there should be freezing mainly at the poles, and the readjustment of the tectonic plates will be great.

-Changing the subject, do you know what the population of the earth is today?

-Do you mean the total number of human individuals?

-There are just over 5 billion living beings and two million three hundred thousand replicants.

-And where does so much energy come from to maintain all this?

-It comes from the sun, of course! Uma answered me.

-Yes, I know that all our energy comes from the Sun, but how is it captured and transferred to the machines?

-There are 3,500 pyramids of varying sizes around the planet that capture energy and distribute it through radiation.

-And there is no other way of capturing and transferring energy?

-In the past it existed, but it fell into disuse because some forms of extraction were potentially dangerous to life, you know, the great administrator is very careful with people's health.

-Great administrator? Which country are you referring to?

-Country? I have no information about that, what is country? I found it strange but for the first time that intelligent machine asked me a question.

-Yes, a kingdom, a domain of any region, what do you call it?

-Dominion of a region, I don't understand, the ten children of the human matrix spread throughout the earth many years ago, but they never determined any region as a domain separate from the whole, they all maintain contact with the central matrix and follow a single guideline that today is dictated by the great administrator.

At that moment I realized that this world was very different from what I knew and I needed to exploit that opportunity to the fullest and find out what had happened to cause that shocking disparity.

-So, to begin with, explain to me what this human matrix is? And the machine patiently explained the following to me.

-A long time ago, humans were formed from the mixture of several similar types and formed a large group gathered on the main continent, the talking beings like you. This group grew and prospered under the guidance of a human who was the most capable, after a few millennia of existence this group was, under the guidance of the ruler of the time, divided and spread around the planet, technological evolution was over the years replacing the governance of humans and to this day life is like this.

And what about this story of the ten children, was there always harmony between them?

-The ten children are not ten individuals, in fact there were ten groups that went out into the world, each one to a different region of the globe.

-I see, and each group formed a separate kingdom.

-No, why would they do that, they are all of the same race, there was never a reason for them to act separately from the central government, even when there was a human in charge.

-Ten groups, and what is the race of these groups?

-The race of talking humans, of course! The machine replied, demonstrating its complete lack of knowledge about human differences.

-Were they all the same skin color?

-According to my information, there are no humans with other skin colors, only black skin like yours.

Mr. "A" was a tall, strong man, with a well-proportioned physique and very dark skin. - And what about religion, did they all follow the same religion? I insisted to see if the machine revealed any reason for the separation of the groups.

-Religion, I don't have information for that, what is religion?

-What was their belief, which God did they believe in? I asked, already with little patience with that machine.

-Yes, all humans believe in a principle of formation, a primordial energy that created all things in seven different stages.

Seven different steps reminded me of the book of Genesis in the Bible, so I thought about asking, I forgot that the machine had access to my thoughts and it continued.

-In the beginning, the universe was only energy. Everything was inanimate, lifeless, calm, silent. The immensity of space was nothingness and darkness. Only the Supreme Spirit, the Great Power, the Creator, the Seven-Headed Serpent existed in this abyss of darkness. He felt the desire to create worlds and created them; he felt the desire to create this planet, inhabited by living beings, and he created it with everything it contains.

-You mentioned seven stages of creation . . .

And the machine continued – Talking animals believe that the creator of everything ordered the following:

1 - That the formless gas scattered throughout space is gathered together to form the planets, and the gas is gathered together in the form of a whirlwind

2 - That the gas solidified to form the planets and the gas then solidified, leaving parts of it to form the waters and the atmosphere; and these volumes of gas enveloped the new world. Darkness reigned and there was no sound, because the atmosphere had not yet been formed, nor the waters.

3 - That the gas from outside separates and forms the atmosphere with the waters: and the gas separated; part of it formed the waters, which spread over the surface of the earth and covered it, although no island appeared. The gas that did not form the waters, became the atmosphere and "the light was included in that atmosphere".

And the rays of the sun met with the rays of light in the atmosphere and formed the day. In this way, light was made. And heat was also included in the atmosphere. "And the rays of the sun met with the rays of heat and brought life.

4 - That the gas which is enclosed within the earth made it rise above the surface of the waters: then the fire from the centre of the earth made the islands and the continents appear, and the waters receded.

5 - Let life appear in the waters: and the rays of the sun met the rays of the earth in the mud of the waters and cosmic eggs (germs of life) were formed among the cells of the mud. And life arose from these cosmic eggs, according to the commandment

6 - Let life appear on earth: and the rays of the sun met with the rays of the earth in the dust and the cosmic eggs were formed; and from these cosmic eggs life emerged, according to the commandment.

7 - Let us create a man in our image and give him the power to take care of the planet and all life on it.

"In this way Narayana, the Seven-Headed Intelligence, the Creator of all things in the universe, created man and placed in his body a living, imperishable spirit, and that animal became an intelligence, like Narayana. And the creation was perfect.

While he was "telling" me all those things, the image in the large aquarium continued to move, the planets rotating around a luminous ball that represented, in a disproportionately smaller way, the Sun.

A beam of light appeared coming from the side of the aquarium and a new caption appeared on the lower part of the side that was in front of me, it was the holographic projection of the radiation of the second Sun. In the image, the fifth planet was being crumbled and spreading all its small particles in a circular orbit, mainly over the small planet next to it.

I had the idea of asking Uma to advance that projection and show me what she calculated would happen to the third blue planet. The image became faster, the little blue planet at a certain point entered the illuminated band, turned a little in the direction of its horizontal axis, a slight inclination and continued on its path in orbit with an inclination, its blue color had also changed, becoming red because of the radiation.

It was a moment of great emotion because I felt proud of that opportunity. Deep down I knew that those were memories of a being who had seen the beginning of an era, that race of talking beings would certainly give rise to humanity as we know it today and all that technology certainly did not remain, leaving only a few traces of their immense works, but life on that planet, the creator that the machine had mentioned, was preserved by His will.

The fourth planet that received a good part of what had been the fifth planet and also suffered from radiation, any life that was there ended in those days and the beam of light suddenly disappeared without reaching all the other bodies because at that moment they were in another period of their orbits.

What had happened to the beam of light that represented the radiation for it to stop? I thought, to which the machine that was connected to my mind promptly answered me.

-The passage of the second Sun will be very quick, the disastrous effects will last a few months, but the changes will remain for a long time, making it impossible for life to overcome this phase. I looked at the hologram and saw that the third globe was once again starting to change color, going from an ochre red to a pink and a few turns later almost completely white while the others maintained their colors with few changes, that is, almost all of them were covered in colored spots, like soap bubbles and the fourth sphere was a bright red because it had absorbed more of that radiation.

"Through the memories of Mr. "A", I plunged into an abyss of sadness and bitterness that few people would dare to imagine today. His life, like that of all the inhabitants of that advanced civilization, was lived in the comfort provided by the most advanced technology that humanity has ever known. However, this comfort was a trap, an illusion that kept them trapped in their own precarious cities, far from the nature that created them.

They lived in virtual isolation, interacting more with holograms and machines than with living beings, disconnected from the natural wonders that once graced the world. The blue sky was replaced by a mixture of radiation from the two suns. This gradual separation from the essence of life consumed them to the core, transforming their existences into an unbearable void. Deprived of purpose and connection, many began to long for their own demise.

That consultation with the hologram was like a dark prelude to the catastrophic outcome that followed. A few days later, a wave of radiation swept through civilization, reducing everything to a rustic, incandescent mass. We thus witnessed the abrupt disappearance of an era whose extraordinary deeds and achievements have been lost in the dust of time.

These beings, endowed with such advanced knowledge that it challenges us to this day, controlled gravity as if it were an extension of their will. Their machines and chemical techniques allowed them to shape solid matter with unimaginable precision and efficiency. The construction of enormous blocks of stone, the enigmatic monoliths that dot our urban landscape, is a mystery that continues to intrigue modern scientists. How was it possible to achieve such a feat without the technological resources we have today? This is a question that echoes through the ages, a solemn echo of the greatness and fall of a civilization that once reigned over the Earth.

But beyond their technological prowess, there was a depth to their understanding of nature and the cosmos that surpassed the limits of our comprehension. They were like gods among mortals, defying the laws of physics and manipulating reality with a dexterity that bordered on the supernatural.

It is impossible not to feel a mixture of admiration and fear at the legacy they left behind, a legacy that encourages us to question our own limitations and dream of what we can still achieve."

After Mr. "A's" memories, I was reminded of a subsequent life in a world where life had not been completely eradicated, unlike on other planets. Thanks to divine intervention, Earth had overcome its near-fatal fate. Humans, referred to by the machine as "talking beings," had managed to survive in deep caves around the globe, giving rise to a new civilization. They still had traces of ancient technology that allowed them to survive and settle in the caves for many years.

The young "B", the protagonist of these memoirs, was a thin and frail boy when he decided to leave his cave for the first time and face the light of day. The climate was hotter and more humid than the environment he was used to underground. A dense forest surrounded the place. Without a traditional family, since he had fled from his group that kept him as a prisoner, "B" was at risk of becoming the meal of those who remained in the cave.

Forced to leave his cave home to fight for survival, "B" found himself alone, as everyone he had grown up with had been devoured by his elders. With little energy left, he managed to reach the surface and wandered through the dense forest, admiring everything he saw in his first experience under the light of day. He stopped near an unknown object, a technological remnant, trying to understand its nature. It was then that a saber-toothed tiger, positioned on top of a large rock, prepared to attack. Innocent and devoid of knowledge of the danger that this creature represented, "B" was paralyzed. A bright ray of lightning shot from the direction he had come from, striking the rock and scaring the tiger away. Momentarily blinded by the intense brightness and frightened, "B" knelt down and lowered his head. Shortly after, he felt a touch on his shoulder.

-Get up, the danger has passed. The beast is gone! Opening his eyes and slowly looking up, "B" saw a man with a unique appearance, unlike anyone he had ever seen. The hunter, robust and between 40 and 50 years old, with dark skin, sported a short beard. He wore a jacket full of pockets containing various objects and held a short spear with two ends, the same weapon that had fired the lightning and scared away the tiger.

Although the young man did not fully understand the events that were unfolding, he decided to follow the man as it seemed to be the only viable option. After a long and arduous journey, they reached a clearing where a peculiar object in the shape of a giant egg with a small side entrance was lying on the ground. The hunter instructed him to wait and entered the object. Minutes later, he emerged carrying a bag from which he took a small package, handing it to the young man "B". Overcome with hunger, "B" recognized it as some kind of food ration and promptly began his meal while watched by the hunter, who sat at the door of the object without saying a word.

"Can you return to your people?" the hunter asked calmly.

- Return? I ran away to avoid being turned into feed; I will never return.

- In that case, come with me. He suggested. Together, they walked to a nearby spring that fell from a modest height — about four meters — forming a small lake before continuing its course as an integral part of the river unknown to "B".

The boy stood there, staring at the hunter, intrigued and not understanding what was happening, amazed, because he had never before witnessed such an abundance of water; all the water he had seen in his short life had been strictly rationed, limited exclusively to essential consumption. The concept of bathing was completely foreign to him. Noticing the young man's confusion, the hunter quickly took him by the arm and positioned him under the continuous flow of the shower.

"Boy," said the hunter with a stern expression, "you are giving off a putrid odor that must be removed immediately; otherwise I cannot take you with me." B was alarmed at being exposed to that icy torrent without clothing, but he quickly began to experience a multitude of new and delightful sensations under that cold, liquid current.

Almost as an automatic reflex to the needs of the current moment and perhaps briefly diverting his thoughts about where he would be taken by the hunter after that necessary initial cleaning.

The man then took something that looked like a sponge from his bag along with a bottle of liquid detergent. After soaking the sponge in the clear solution provided by the bottle, he handed it to B, instructing him firmly: "Use this to clean yourself." As he ran the scrubbing sponge over his teenage body, he suddenly noticed his skin take on a different tone as he watched stubborn layers – be they dye or accumulated debris – dissolve, forming deep brown stains in the water below him.

After an hour of meticulously scrubbing himself, B realized that the hunter had moved away without him noticing. When he got out of the water and stopped to the side, B noticed that his skin color was different from that of his rescuer – while the hunter's skin was black, his was white. This fact deeply surprised B, leading him to wonder if his color had changed because of the water, since he had never imagined that there could be so much water capable of forming such a river and allowing for such a comprehensive bath.

While waiting for his friend to return, B put his hands back in the water and took the opportunity to drink. Moments later, the hunter returned and calmly handed the boy a vial containing a special liquid: "Rub well and then rinse." They watched together as B washed away all of his dyed hair until it revealed its original long red strands. Curiously, they did not know why B had previously been covered in a muddy substance on his body; after removing it, he emerged not only physically different from the black boy originally rescued by the hunter from the clutches of a wild beast — but as a completely transformed creature.

– Put this on, they'll come and rescue us before nightfall. He said as he handed over a shirt. However, B didn't know how to put it on because he had never worn such a piece of clothing before; so the hunter quickly helped him with the process. Then, they both returned to the place where the device had fallen and waited for help.

At the end of that afternoon, already next to the faulty device, they saw the rescue that came, as the hunter called it, in the form of a large vimana, a flying machine in the shape of a disc the size of a sports court or about sixty meters in diameter and six meters high, with many windows around it. The device hovered in the air without any noise at a height of ten meters, and with its shadow it darkened the place, opening a passage in the floor through which a metal ladder descended that did not touch the ground.

- Climb up, I'll come right after you. Said the hunter, ordering B to climb onto the device.

B, who was used to stairs, as there were many in the large cave where he was born, quickly climbed up onto the device, while the hunter climbed slowly, showing some difficulty due to his age.

The ladder started from the ceiling of the second floor of the device, so that at the end of the climb B was already inside the machine, staying next to it while the hunter finished his climb. When he looked to the side he saw that it was a room without devices and there were other people waiting for them to arrive.

The hunter had just climbed up and jumped into the ship. As soon as he let go of the ladder, it began to be retracted. One of the men in the ship, a strange-looking man, had skin a little lighter than the hunter's and a long white beard with few hairs, and was wearing what appeared to be a beige linen robe. Probably the oldest man there, he walked up to the hunter and greeted him with his hands together in a prayer gesture.

- Welcome! The hunter repeated the gesture, greeting the host and said

- I found this little boy lost in the forest, as I know that there are no conditions for him to survive here, I brought him with me.

The old man looked at B and turned to the hunter and said – He is an intraterrestrial, we have heard of them a few times. And are you a survivor?

The hunter smiled and said – I am the son of a survivor, when the lands were swallowed I was not born.

- Yes, that was many years ago. The old man argued and continued, - We are doing reconnaissance because many specimens of living creatures have appeared on the planet, have you seen many beings on your ship?

- Yes, I flew over a region where there were some giants, but that was very far from here, and to the north there are some islands where there are beings that are half men and half four-legged animals, they have 4 legs and two arms.

- During a flight over a remote region to the south, I observed the presence of gigantic figures, although this location is significantly distant from our current area. Additionally, to the north, there are islands where hybrid creatures with both human and animalistic characteristics reside; specifically, these beings have four legs and two arms.

The room where B was inside the ship was a round room approximately 4 meters in diameter, with a trapdoor in the center where the ladder had descended. Around it, there was a bench that circled almost the entire room. While the commander and the hunter were talking, a door opened and another hairy man like the others, wearing the same type of clothing that seemed to be a uniform, called the host. It was evident that the commander of the ship was the tall, hairy man, as he was approached by the man who spoke in a language unknown to B and the hunter. The atmosphere in that round room was full of mystery and expectation, leaving the two visitors intrigued about what was to come. Soon everyone went out through the corridor that led to a panoramic room from where they could see the dense forest and the river with a dark appearance.

After a long flight over the forest, the same crew member who had previously led us to the lounge spoke to the captain in his own language before leaving. The captain then exchanged a few words with the hunter and led us to a different crew compartment. In this new environment, we were offered a generous lunch consisting of a variety of fruits, grains and seeds. Before starting the meal, the captain bowed, which B interpreted as a gesture of gratitude; he then sat down at the table with the hunter and the young man.

- I don't understand, but several different creatures have appeared all over the earth. The commander told the hunter.

The hunter's expression changed abruptly upon hearing the commander, showing that he had some relevant information. Then he tilted his head, adopted a reflective posture and, resting his chin on his hand, replied:

- Regrettably, I am aware that it was the genetic alterations made by my people that caused these consequences. In an attempt to adapt and survive the radiation coming from the second Sun, we sought to strengthen our people, which inadvertently resulted in the creation of a wide variety of creatures, including giants. It is with regret that I state that one of these giants was responsible for my father's death.

As the craft continued its high speed westward, the evening became longer than usual. As it approached Atlantis, the ship slowed down to allow a closer look at the island. Located in a marshy, flooded area, Atlantis was characterized by several concentric flooded rings, with the outermost circle extending over 50 kilometers. The ship stopped at a good height just before the first circle so that we could see the entire city, and the captain decided that we would spend the night there.

Before leaving, the Commander showed the guests the cabin where the young man and the hunter would be accommodated.

This was located next to a side door that led to the corridor of the observation room where young B spent a considerable period admiring the beautiful city, notably the imposing marble statues all in sensual poses, which demarcated the place. He also observed that in the inner circle there were only four statues and that the outermost circle was full of those monuments, all in different poses.

After some time the commander arrived and addressed the boy for the first time.

- Enjoying seeing Poseidon's kingdom? Know that it's not just this island, there are others to the north

- I've never seen anything like it, I didn't even know there were so many people in the world.

- There are a few more cities but this is the biggest of them all.

- There are many things I don't understand in this world, I lived a long time underground and we never knew anything about the surface. The commander thought it was funny as if it were a joke, and the boy continued - The other day I was talking about my friend being a survivor, what did he survive?

- How long have you known him?

- I met him the day we were rescued by you. The room they were in was empty, with large windows that went from the ceiling to almost the floor, so the commander sat with his legs crossed and motioned for the young man to sit next to him and began to tell the story.

- Many years ago, I wasn't even born when the great catastrophe happened. Another planetary system passed very close to ours, practically collided, and some planets were completely destroyed, ours suffered from the impact and a large portion of land was submerged, which still causes many problems for us today. Your people, for example, went to the caves to escape the effects of this collision and never came out again.

- True, no one there knows about the existence of the world out here.

- The portion of land where life began was called the mother, and it was the main place on earth, everything was centralized there, but it was destroyed in a short time, leaving only the children, that is, the colonies, which ended up separating and becoming other kingdoms; soon one kingdom will begin to try to dominate the other.

- There are many things that I can't understand in this story, what are planets? And how can the Earth sink?

- You've seen the Sun, for sure! It doesn't hang up there like that light over there. The commander pointed to the lamp in the center of the observation room.

- No! Then how does he stay here?

- It stays there flying in empty space and we are circling it along with ten other planets.

-And they never hit each other?

- Wait a moment, I'll be right back. The commander stood up with silent determination and crossed the room with quick, precise steps. The curious gaze followed him until he disappeared beyond the door.

Minutes later, the commander returned with the same promptness with which he had left. His expression was unperturbed, but his eyes shone with restrained energy.

When he resumed his seat, his hands were busy, each holding a small cylindrical object. The suspense heightened as he displayed them briefly before continuing his narrative.

- Look at this, if you bring these two pieces together, one will push the other, but if you turn one side, they will attract each other. He said as he placed the pieces on the floor of the ship, demonstrating, then asked the young man to hold them and repeat the demonstration.

- So the Sun doesn't fall because of that? And this machine flying at such a height, is that why it doesn't fall either?

- More or less, in fact we are all falling, the Sun and the planets are falling into the void of space, one next to the other at great speed.

-I see, the Sun and Earth are falling in space, but the machine remains suspended because of this effect.

- Exactly! - And how do you manage not to get lost? You have no way of marking the path so you can return to your starting point. How do you do that? Asked the curious young man.

- I can show you a few things. In many places, we use markers on the ground that point to the desired location and direction. When we can't see these landmarks, like when we're flying over the sea or when they're too far away, we use the sky to guide us, looking at the stars.

B looked up and saw the starry night above them, then looked at the circles of Atlantis and thought that the statues could serve to indicate the direction – Now go to sleep, tomorrow I will show you how we always manage to know our location.

The next morning one of the crew members brought a meal and said something that neither the hunter nor B could understand because the crew members did not speak the same language as them. Then they went out to the room with the windows. The day had already dawned and illuminated the ship, which, due to its height, cast a small shadow on the field near the city. The commander soon arrived in that room and made his usual greeting. The hunter and the young man reciprocated in the same way.

- If you want to stay here in this kingdom, you can disembark there, but if you want to continue, you need to know that this is a circumnavigation voyage. The commander said as he pointed to a small circle of stones on the ground. In a few days we will be back in our kingdom and starting point. Our objective is to observe the new species and make a reconnaissance trip.

- I don't know this place and my ship will certainly not be repaired, it is very old and can no longer store energy, so if you can do us the honor of following this mission, I will help in whatever way is necessary. - And you, white man! He asked young B.

- I want to stay and learn how to navigate. I was born and lived in a cave that is surrounded by a forest. I had never seen a city like this before, and I never imagined it existed. B replied.

- So let's go ahead, we have more than a day across the ocean to the next island, I'll provide uniforms, introduce you to the rest of the ship and the crew. You can make yourself at home, I'll be right back.

And the ship began its journey, passing gently over the Atlantic, then headed west over the sea, increasing its speed almost imperceptibly. After some time, the captain returned to the cabin and brought uniforms for B and the hunter. Upon entering the cabin, he placed the clothes on the table in the corner of the small room.

- Is that a vajra? He asked as he picked up the object that looked like a two-pronged indigenous spear.

- Yes, but it doesn't work anymore, I no longer have the energy to activate it, my batteries ran out when I scared away the tiger that was going to attack the young white man.

- Can you leave him with me?

- Of course, take the batteries too. The hunter replied as he handed him the old jacket that was placed on the floor next to him. The commander left the cabin taking the spear and the jacket with the batteries.

Soon after, B and the hunter put on their uniforms and went to the observation room. They realized that, during the night, the ship had crossed the sea and was now flying over a dense forest. Suddenly, the vimana slowed down, and they both saw a creature that was clearly a giant, as it was almost twice the size of most of the trees around it. As they got closer, they realized that it was a machine, a robot of colossal size, that was walking towards the mountains. The ship followed at a short distance, enough so that it could not be reached or even noticed by whoever was operating the device.

The robot continued walking through the valley, climbing higher and higher until it reached an area where only the rock of the mountain was exposed, with several more robots working on the site. The hunter and B, aboard the vimana hovering about 50 meters above the ground, were watching the movement of the machines when the commander arrived and gave his customary greeting, which was immediately reciprocated by B and the hunter.

-I see you are observing the construction machines! The great ape man spoke excitedly as he approached the window, and continued – They are relics of the past era that are still producing stone artifacts. The inhabitants here want to build a new supply center. Look at the steps they have already made for cultivation. The commander spoke and pointed to the nearby mountain, on the other side of the valley, where there was a series of platforms forming a kind of enormous staircase that only a giant could climb up those steps. Above the great staircase, they had also started construction with large walls, probably for land containment.

The construction machine, which had a humanoid shape, lay down and a small door opened on its left side. A short man with medium dark skin came out of it. He turned to the vimana and saluted in the same way the commander always did.

- Let's go down, that man needs our help! The ape man exclaimed urgently. Without wasting any time, he left the room, returning a few minutes later. In his hands, he carried the hunter's jacket and the vajra, as well as a small electronic device, which was kept in a bag with a very short strap.

The ape man handed the jacket and vajra to the hunter. "I managed to recharge your batteries," the commander said as the hunter quickly put on the jacket, adjusting it to his body. The commander told another crew member to open the trapdoor and everyone headed to the central room, where a trapdoor began to open with a soft creak. The ladder leading to the outside of the ship slowly appeared, extending until it almost touched the ground.

With the ship hovering just a few feet above the ground, the descent was not as difficult as they had feared. The ape-man descended first, his movements agile and precise, followed closely by the hunter, who, despite the weight of his jacket and vajra, moved with determination. They crossed the short distance between the ship and the ground quickly, their eyes alert for any sign of danger.

As they touched the ground, they both prepared to face whatever was waiting for them, aware that the help they would provide could be crucial to the survival of the man they had seen in trouble.

The machine operator arrived and began to converse with the commander in a local language that neither B nor the hunter could understand. However, the ape man was able to follow the conversation thanks to the small electronic device he carried, which translated the unknown language.

The device was remarkable, emitting a faint glow as it processed and translated the words. Even though B and the hunter did not understand the translated language, the ape man listened intently, absorbing every detail of the conversation.

The discussion between the machine operator and the commander went on for several minutes. Facial expressions and gestures revealed that the matter was of great importance. The commander, who initially seemed calm, began to show increasing concern as the conversation progressed.

Finally, after a long exchange of words, the commander turned to the group. His face was tense, and his eyes reflected deep concern. He sighed, ready to share what he had learned with the operator, aware that the news could change the course of their actions.

- Let's go back! The commander ordered and everyone climbed aboard and after climbing the ladder the ship began to head north.

-We need to act quickly because they are on the verge of going to war with another group. The commander spoke as the ship increased its speed and altitude, and continued. - You saw the machines working, they transform the stone into a kind of paste with a chemical that melts any type of rock, then the machines scrape the stone and carry the paste to the other mountain and place it in molds made with panels that are assembled on site.

- I know, I've seen them make huge blocks. The hunter replied.

- And do you know the chemistry that melts the rock? Asked the monkey man.

- I know it's made with a mixture of herbs and urine from some animal species, but I've never seen how it's made.

- Well, here they have some specimens that provide the urine to make the preparation. But they were all kidnapped by another tribe, so the builders are preparing to fight because they think it was the centaurs who kidnapped the animals. I promised the chief builder that I would bring him some specimens and solve the problem. I asked him to wait for me for four days.

- What about the vegetable mix, do they have it?

- The centaurs are also the ones who supply it, that's why they think the centaurs want their end, there is no harmony or understanding there between the builders and the guardians of the forests, one blames the other, if I don't intervene it will be the end of both. While we don't reach our destination, come with me, let's eat and then I'll show you the rest of the ship. Having said that, the commander called the hunter and young B who followed him to the dining room where they sat at a table near a window from where they could see a dense forest with some rivers that ran through small valleys.

The vimana flew silently and at great speed. After the meal, the ape man called B and the hunter to see the interior of the ship. They started in the dining room, which had a door connected to the main corridor and a side exit that gave access to a large semi-circular hall. This hall took up almost the entire space of the vimana and housed four generator sets responsible for supplying power to the machine.

Several workers were busy making sure everything was working perfectly. The soft sound of the machines and the glow of the lights indicated the efficiency of the system. At the end of the hall, there was a circular staircase that led to the upper floor, where the commander led them.

On the upper floor they found a large pantry and several other compartments, all arranged lengthwise except for the ladder mechanism, which could be lowered to the ground when necessary, located in the center of the ship. The commander, with determined steps, led the way, explaining the function of each area.

He mentioned a small compartment on the upper deck, highlighting that it was where the navigation center was located. This room operated everything automatically and was directly linked to the commander's thoughts, transforming the vimana into a nearly autonomous machine. The ship, guided by the commander, was able to respond instantly to his mental commands, demonstrating the incredible technology and integration of the system.

As they explored, the ape man watched B and the hunter's reactions closely, aware that the complexity and sophistication of the vimana probably surpassed anything they had ever seen before.

At the end of the demonstration, they returned to the observation room and saw a sunny afternoon as they flew over the sea. The craft began to slow down and decrease in altitude, gliding smoothly through the sky. Soon, they spotted a peninsula ahead.

On the peninsula, a small pyramid appeared on the horizon. As they approached it, they saw that it was an impressive structure, with a square base and nine levels, rising to about 30 meters in height. Each side of the pyramid had a central staircase that led to the top, where there was a square space.

The craft continued to slow down and hovered over the pyramid, remaining at a distance of approximately 3 meters above the top and descended its ladder to disembark at that location.

- Let's go down!" said the ape man in a firm tone, heading towards the stairwell room. Everyone was waiting in the access room, attentive and a little tense. The commander, with his authoritative presence, looked at young B. He made a thoughtful expression and, in his rude way, said: "You stay here and await my orders!"

The commander was the first of the group to descend to the stone square at the top of the pyramid, his footsteps echoing heavily. Behind him, the hunter, ever vigilant, followed swiftly. The crewman, a little hesitant, was next. As soon as the crewman stepped onto the spot, a deep, thunderous sound echoed through the surroundings. The earth began to shake violently, as if the pyramid were alive and angry. The crewman lost his balance and fell to the floor below. He narrowly avoided rolling to the ground down the steep stairs, but remained there, motionless and bleeding, his face contorted in pain.

The commander's voice sounded clear and authoritative in young B's mind, ordering him to go to the cabin to get a specific device, similar to a flashlight, that emitted a healing light. B ran through the corridors of the ship, his heart beating fast with adrenaline. He knew that every second counted.

While B was in the cabin, the ship moved smoothly, descending the ladder to be near the fallen crewman. The soft light of the ship bathed the environment, giving a surreal tone to the scene. Upon returning to the ladder room, the commander again communicated mentally with B, instructing him to descend with the device.

Carefully, B walked down the stairs to the injured crewman. The captain was already kneeling beside the injured man, his expression intent. As soon as B handed over the device, the captain began to shine the light from the flashlight on the crewman's leg. The light was bright but gentle, and seemed to pulse with its own energy. Gradually, the bleeding began to slow, and the pained expression on the crewman's face softened a little.

On the ground, some local residents watched the scene with wide eyes. They watched in amazement as the crew member got up after a few minutes, without pain or bleeding, completely recovered from the fall. Their murmurs of surprise echoed through the air. Their attention then turned to the descent of the occupants of the great vimana down the stairs of the pyramid, an impressive and almost mystical sight. The locals could not believe what they were seeing; the miraculous recovery and descent of the strange occupants of the vimana needed to be brought to everyone's attention.

Soon a man appeared who seemed to be the leader of the group, as he was already known to the commander. They greeted each other familiarly, exchanging quick and firm words, before heading towards a nearby building. The atmosphere was charged with tension, as if the earth sensed what was to come. Before they could enter the building, the earth began to shake violently. This time, the tremors were much more intense and lasting than before. The buildings shook, dust and rocks fell from above, and the ground seemed to undulate like the sea in a storm.

That day, a series of violent tremors shook the entire region, continuing until the next morning, as if the creator himself wanted to prevent the ape-man's success in preventing the impending war between the builders and the centaurs. The night was a torment of deafening noises and constant vibrations, preventing any possibility of rest.

When the sun finally rose the next day, the leader of the group, the commander, and another crew member of the vimana went out to check on the wounded. The streets were littered with debris and the air was thick with dust. They ordered the hunter and young B to wait in the ship. The hunter, a man with piercing eyes and wiry muscles, nodded with a serious expression. Young B, still stunned by the events, remained silent, but his eyes showed concern.

They spent the day on the ship, in the company of other crew members, monitoring the situation and awaiting instructions. The wait was agonizing, each minute dragging on like an eternity. The occasional sound of minor tremors and the restless murmurs of the crew created an atmosphere of continuous tension.

The next morning, after a restless night full of apprehension, the hunter turned to young B and said in a resolute tone - White, let's go and see what happened.

Young B looked at the hunter, his determination reflected in the older man's eyes. They knew that despite the danger, they needed to understand the extent of the damage and how they could help. With one last look at the relative safety of the ship, they both prepared to face whatever awaited them outside.

They soon found the chief of the tribe and the commander hard at work treating the wounded. The monkey man, with his magic lantern, was recovering the wounded. Broken arms and legs were healed in a matter of minutes, cuts healed immediately, and those who recovered brought more people from that group, who lived in simple houses in the middle of the forest.

Little by little, the makeshift tents began to empty. The frantic rhythm of the ape man's hands, coupled with the healing light from his lantern, seemed almost supernatural. The gratitude in the eyes of the healed wounded was undeniable, and the people around began to look at the ape man with reverence and respect.

After a few hours of hard work, there were no more injuries. The last person to be cured was a child, who had been crying in pain from a broken leg. Now he ran happily among the adults, showing off his fully recovered leg.

The chief of the tribe, without hesitation, ordered the animals to be brought. Shortly after, a pair of llamas with completely white fur were presented. Handing them over to the ape man, the chief spoke a few more words in the strange language and the two conversed for a few minutes. The vimana, with an almost imperceptible movement, began to move.

The commander, exhausted but relieved, looked around and saw that peace had been restored to the small community. He then made his way to the small lake nearby, where the calm waters offered a calming contrast to the recent chaos. He saluted the local deity and returned to a platform near the pyramid where the vimana stood. The sun was beginning to set, tinting the sky with shades of orange and pink, and those who had been healed followed suit.

From the top of the small platform near the pyramid, he gave a brief farewell speech in the local language, uttering words of peace and unity among them all. Then, together with the hunter and the crewman, he returned to the vimana. As soon as they entered, the ship began to slowly rise, and after gaining a little more altitude, it began its journey back to the builders' site.

Slowly, the ladder was raised and a rectangular metal basket was lowered from the ship. Carefully, the llamas were placed inside the basket and hoisted into the ship. Then the ape man, the ship's crewman, the hunter and the young white man climbed into the same cargo basket, which was lowered again to retrieve them, completing the process with mechanical precision.

The vimana slowly began to turn and gain altitude, with the setting sun to the right of the observation room. Soon, it began its trajectory towards the builders' site.

The ship traveled all night, flying over the sea and many mountains. The next morning, it stopped its course and began to descend, reaching about ten meters from the ground of the quarry where the giant machines had worked days before. B, who had spent the entire night in the observation room, realized that something was wrong, because all the machines had disappeared.

The commander entered the room, made the usual greeting, approached the large window and watched as if watching a film. "Let's go further," said the ape man, and the ship continued its course towards the south.

Minutes later, as it flew over a large lake high in the mountains, its speed began to slow down again. Finally, the ship stopped near another unfinished construction site. Several blocks of stone were scattered on the ground, and the machines, those giant robots that transformed the stones into a concrete-like mass, were partially dismantled and thrown into the field ahead, as if they had been destroyed by an overwhelming force. The scene was desolate, with pieces of metal and fragments of stone mixed together in apparent chaos.

B felt a chill as he contemplated the scene. "What happened here?" he muttered, more to himself than to the others. The ape man remained silent, his gaze fixed on the remains of the unfinished work. "We need to investigate," the commander finally said, breaking the silence. "There is more going on than meets the eye."

The ship hovered for a few more moments, as the crew tried to absorb the magnitude of the destruction beneath them. The ape man and the hunter exchanged a meaningful look, a silent communication that indicated they both knew this discovery would change the course of their mission. Slowly, the vimana began to descend the ladder once more, this time with renewed purpose to unravel the mysteries that awaited them below.

After the monkey man with his bag, the hunter carrying his vajra, the crew member and young B, the four pathfinders descended, the ladder was collected, and the group continued towards the remains of the building. The structure looked like a pile of dismantled building pieces.

One of the wrecks the group headed for was a large block of stone, measuring approximately 3.5 meters high by about 4 meters wide, with a central doorway. The doorway was quite low, and the commander would have had difficulty crossing it without stooping.

Suddenly, a small man appeared through the passage, belonging to the same tribe as the builders. He passed easily through the door, holding an object in his hand. The hunter, without hesitation, pointed his vajra and fired a bolt that would have cut the man in half. However, the commander, with quick reflexes, pushed the hunter's arm up, deflecting the shot, which left only a cut in the stone portal that was almost a meter thick.

The man, who was holding a piece of metal in his hand as if it were a weapon, threw himself to the ground, dropping the tool and covering his face, terrified of his near-fatal fate. His wide eyes and trembling body revealed the terror he felt at realizing how close he had come to death. The group was silent for a moment, absorbing the intensity of what had happened.

Slowly the group approached him. The hunter extended his hand to help him up, showing in a gesture his regret for the instinctive shot. The man, accepting the help, began to speak in that strange language. The commander quickly activated his translator device, so that everyone could hear.

"...then, after the destruction of the machines, new lands appeared down there. Everyone went there, fleeing the disease and exploring the new lands." This was what the hunter and the young White man understood.

— New lands have emerged where, in which direction? — asked the ape man, his deep voice echoing across the terrain.

—The messenger came from this direction. — said the builder, pointing to the west.

— And the centaurs, how are they? — asked the commander, concern evident on his face.

—I think they all died from the mysterious disease. — replied the builder, his voice full of sadness and resignation.

"Let's leave the animals we brought here and go with the vimana to see these new lands," the commander said, his determination clear in every word. He looked at the hunter, who nodded silently.

Soon, the basket with the animals began to be lowered from the ship. The group watched in silence as the animals, frightened and curious, stepped onto the new terrain. The hunter, with a distant look, pondered the fate of the centaurs and the new lands that were emerging. The young White, at his side, tried to absorb all the information, feeling more and more a part of this extraordinary journey.

The commander, determined, turned to the group. "We have a mission. Let's see these new lands and then continue our journey," he said, his firm voice inspiring confidence.

The ape man, the builder, the hunter and the young White man exchanged looks of determination. They knew that this journey would be dangerous, but also full of opportunities and discoveries.

With the vimana hovering just a few feet above the ground again, the group prepared to depart. Curiosity and hope guided their steps as they left behind the animals they had brought with them, searching for answers in the unknown lands they would later travel to.

— Doesn't the worthy King have any concerns about placing these animals here? They could be killed by the mysterious disease that decimated the centaurs — said the builder to the ape man.

The monkey man became thoughtful and looked towards the lake, as if seeing something invisible to the common eyes. After a few minutes, he calmly turned to the hunter.

— Take the animals out of the basket and give them to this man. Then we will go and get some treatment for them.

The hunter walked to the basket, removed the animals and returned to the place, accompanied by the pair of llamas. He handed them over to the builder.

— Take good care of this couple, they are very young. — The commander's translator worked immediately, providing understanding to the builder, who approached the couple and caressed both of them, who showed no fear or any reaction.

The commander turned off his device and spoke to the builder in the local language. Then they returned to the ship in the basket, and the builder left with the llamas.

The vimana continued slowly, floating towards the ocean and decreasing its altitude. It passed through some clouds until it reached a few meters above the sea and turned on its own axis, placing the observation room facing the great wall that was the mountain range, today known as the Andes. Above the clouds, the layer of snow that partially covered that land was visible, and below the few clouds, the new lands that had emerged.

—That man called you King, is that true? — the boy asked the commander.

— Yes! I am King. That is how they recognize me in my lands — replied the monkey man.

—And why didn't you keep that weapon that shoots lightning? Didn't the hunter give it to you?

— Simple. That is the most powerful weapon that exists at this time, but it is still a weapon of destruction and, for me, it is of no use. My weapon emits a light that repairs damage; it does not destroy things, it has the power to heal.

The ape man paused, looking at the new lands that had appeared in front of the mountain range. His voice took on a deeper, more reflective tone.

— Look at our planet. Many years ago, it suffered a magnetic impact that caused the destruction of an entire continent and almost all life. That continent that was submerged will provoke several reactions for a few eons until everything calms down. For example, I notice here that those lands rose a lot, but in the near future, nothing will be remembered, not even the existence of the lands that are gone. Our stay here in this body is very brief at this time, my function is to preserve life. That is why I am here with you. But know that many species will not survive for long. In truth, everything passes. Everything that is alive is temporary, even this planet. Only the source that creates the worlds is eternal and can always be observed by feelings, at any time, in any place in the universe.

— The same way it happened with the centaurs? — asked the young White, his voice full of curiosity mixed with sadness.

The ape man nodded slowly, his eyes reflecting the wisdom accumulated through the ages.

— Yes, just like the centaurs. They were also part of this cycle. But just as their cycle ended, new cycles begin. And it is our duty to ensure that new cycles have a chance to flourish.

The young White looked at the commander, understanding the depth of his words. The vimana continued to float gently over the sea, casting a golden glow over the waters.

The next morning the ship continued its flight over the ocean, following that mountain range in the distance and then passing to the other side of the mountain range, changing direction, heading east again and flying over the dense forest again until it saw an area where there were several sets of circular buildings made of stone and with a dome-shaped roof forming groups of three circles spaced at a good distance that, seen from above, seemed to be a few kilometers apart, separating each group.

The vimana stopped near the first group of tents, flying at an altitude of about fifty meters or more, and everyone saw several beings bathing in a river that ran alongside those tents. They were all similar, and there were tall men, but they only had a torso and limbs, missing a head. They still had a small area of hair in place of a neck. They were bathing naked, males and females. When they saw the vimana, they all left, trying to hide inside the tents.

The young White man and the hunter looked at the commander, all frightened by the scene, "Let's go and see the other group." The ape man spoke with determination and the ship slowly passed over those buildings and continued on to the next group. As we flew over the next group of circular buildings we saw that some of those headless beings were working on the land, starting some cultivation because there was a small area where the forest had been cleared for cultivation. In the same way, everyone ran away in fear into their tents and the vimana continued on to the third group.

When we reached the third group, there was a small clearing in the forest next to the buildings, and the vimana stopped above, reducing its altitude so that it could descend. However, we did not see the beings, only the buildings. "Let's go down!" said the commander, and the hunter left the room to get his weapon, while the White Man and the monkey man went to the descent room. The descent basket came out of the upper part of the room, and a passage opened on the floor for the group to descend. Without any delay, the three were taken to the ground.

Next to where the basket was lowered there was a tree and some bushes. From the middle of the foliage someone shot an arrow at the monkey man who with impressive agility caught it in the air before it hit him in the chest. The hunter promptly aimed his vajra, ready to fire a ray, but there was no visible target so he stopped and everyone remained alert for a few seconds until another arrow appeared in his direction which he struck with a ray causing it to disintegrate in the air. Then a third arrow met the same end and the hunter fired another ray that penetrated the bush in the direction where the third arrow had come from and certainly hit a target.

Then a creature came out from the side of the bush, holding his bow with his hands raised above his body and in a sort of surrender, he knelt a few meters in front of the hunter and threw the bow at his feet.

That being who didn't produce any sound, somehow transmitted his distress and fear to the group, remained there, kneeling with his arms stretched out in front of him without moving – Get up! exclaimed the commander and the translator emitted an incomprehensible sound.

The commander and the hunter looked at each other and the ape man went to the place where the being had come from, the headless man and saw another being, visibly younger, was lying on the ground, the lifeless body with a large burn caused by the ray that passed through the middle of the chest hitting the mouth which was at the height of the heart and continuing until close to the right eye which was close to the armpit.

When the Commander saw this, he immediately said, "Harapa, go to the ship and get my device. Let's see if this one works." The hunter went back to the basket, climbed into the vimana, and a few minutes later returned with the monkey man's flashlight. He immediately began to shine a blue light on the creature's wound, magically making the burn disappear, but the creature didn't move. Then he stood up and declared the job finished, "Let's go, because we can't expect anything from them!" And he signaled for them to return to the vimana basket. The creature that had come to them was still crouched down with its arms outstretched on the ground.

After arriving at the observation room - Look who's going there! Exclaimed the hunter, amazed at the scene in which he saw the creatures, the one that had surrendered and the one that had not gotten up after the burn was restored, walking together, returning to the building embraced, as if nothing had happened.

- That's the big problem they have, they are very ashamed and afraid of being different from other creatures, they avoid contact and interaction with other species as much as possible. The commander spoke with his great wisdom.

The vimana rose a few meters and began its journey north, increasing its speed until it flew over the sea. After sunset, everyone went to the dining room to eat and then returned to their cabins.

The next morning, the commander called the hunter and his companion Branco to the viewing room because the ship had begun to lose altitude. It continued flying over the sea until it reached a few meters above the surface of the water and continued its flight east until it reached a beach. It advanced a few meters to escape the reach of the tide and stopped at a slightly higher location where it was then forced to lower the support columns and finally make a final landing and the entire crew descended, in total there were 12 crew members, six dark-skinned men and six of the same race as the commander, in addition to the hunter and the young Branco.

-- The main generator stopped and the others could not support the load because they were also weak. Said one of the crew members, of the same race as the commander, he was a tall and very strong guy who wore a leather jacket over his uniform.

The commander divided the group, ordering the dark brown men to build a furnace and then stay in the vimana and the rest to follow him, the hunter and the young White in search of minerals to repair the ship.

It was a plain with some pine trees and the group went ahead until, as they passed a pine tree, a being similar to a werewolf attacked the commander who was in front of the group. The creature jumped and tried to bite the ape man in the neck, but received a blow that threw him a few meters away. When he fell, he got up and launched another attack that was again repelled by the ape man's speed. The hunter, with his weapon, prepared to fire a ray, could do nothing due to the risk of hitting the commander. Two other beings with dog faces appeared and were repelled by the ray fired by the hunter, and the first attacker fell unconscious.

The other two fled and minutes later returned to the attack accompanied by about five more, but before any action the hunter fired a ray and thus ended the scene that ended with two dead beings with large burns, thus silencing the entire attack.

The surviving beings stood still, frightened by the smell of burning flesh and without action in front of the group, until the commander in front of the group and with his translation device spoke to the attackers.

-- My group and I came in peace but we can exterminate you immediately, do you have a leader?

The dog-headed being that had been knocked down by the ape man and was lying to the side, began to get up, kneeling down, began to speak and the commander's device translated. -- I am the leader of this group! What do you want here? We will not attack you anymore, but I want to know what you are looking for.

-- We need to fix our transport, I need some minerals, some certain bright blue stones.

The leader of the dog-headed men made a signal and the others picked up those who had been shot by the hunter and carried them away, leaving only the leader who spoke to the ape man.

-- I'll get what you need and you can go!

-- Yes, we only need two or three days to make the repairs and we will leave. The commander replied.

The dog-head began to walk through the pine forest, the hunter and the young white man followed the group with some difficulty and only stopped at the edge of a stream when it was starting to get dark.

-- On the other side of this stream, a little further ahead, there is a tribe that has what you are looking for. Take advantage of the night and steal the material you want. Said the dog head.

--No, we will never do that! The ape man replied, knowing that his crew would agree with him.

-- Tell that one over there to finish off their race and it will all be yours! The canine insisted, referring to the hunter with the ray gun.

-- I will go there and talk to them, the White Man will go with me. The hunter volunteered.

So the young White man and the hunter, taking the commander's translator and his gun, crossed the stream while the six ape men and the dog-headed leader sat waiting for their return.

After a few minutes of walking, they saw the tribe and stopped behind a pine tree. "Here, put on my jacket and hold this!" said the hunter, handing the jacket and the ray gun to the young White man.

– But how do you use it? White asked.

--It's easy, you hold it by the middle, place one end on the jacket and point it at your target, use your concentration and press firmly and it will do the rest, releasing a ray for as long as you want. But be careful, this is one of the most powerful weapons in existence.

The young man sat leaning against the pine tree while the hunter left. He saw a figure of the same height as the hunter approach him from some distance and then continue walking. White remained there, alone, in the midst of all the darkness of the forest, remembering the time he lived in a cave, grateful for finding a friend who trusted him with his life and his weapon.

The day had already dawned when the hunter returned accompanied by four other tribesmen, each of them carrying a bag of blue minerals. They went up the river and met up with the rest of the group. Branco noticed that the men who accompanied them were not of the same race because they had legs similar to those of horses and oxen. One who looked like the oldest still had two small horns on his forehead, but the young man preferred to remain silent, after all, it was not the first different being he had encountered and this was the original objective of the trip.

When they reached the place where they had initially crossed the stream, the hunter waved to his companions who placed their loads on the ground and, after a wave to the hunter, returned to their tribe. After they had disappeared from sight, the hunter took the gun and told Branco to go and call the monkey men on the other side of the stream to fetch the load.

The ape men who were hiding behind pine trees came to collect the cargo. The wolf man who had led them to that place was amazed at the amount of minerals obtained by the hunter.

--How did you get all this? Asked the wolf man when he saw the leather bags with all the mineral.

-- It was easy, I told the truth, that I had hit two of you to the chief of the tribe and he gave me this and even told me to help me bring it here

-- We live at war with them because of this mineral and they give it to a stranger who is of another race, of course you threatened them with your weapon!

-- No! It wasn't necessary, he was so pleased when I said I had hit two of his friends that he gave me the ore I asked for. Everyone laughed when they heard the hunter's answer and the wolf man, unable to do anything, lowered his ears in shame. - Let's stop the war, we won't have any more fights between our tribes. And the group returned to the vimana, while the wolf man went determinedly to his tribe.

Upon reaching the ship, the hunter took the lead without hesitation. His firm voice ordered the ape men to immediately begin preparing the minerals needed to repair the machine. The urgency in his tone was clear: they needed to get out of this place as soon as possible. The ape men, always efficient and precise, began to transform all the raw material into fine sand, carrying it up to the top floor of the vimana in a joint effort. Hours turned into days, and during that time, Harapa kept his attention fixed on the work of processing the materials. After three days of tireless dedication, he finally had what he needed.

With the refined material in his hands, the hunter carried it to the furnace that the crew had improvised outside the ship. The smelting process was meticulous, and Harapa oversaw every detail with the watchful eye of a master of his craft. By the end of this arduous process, he had created six perfectly shaped metal disks, each one shining with the gleam of hard-won success. These disks were installed into the vimana's generators, which soon began to vibrate gently, as if awakening from a long slumber. The familiar sound of the machines coming to life echoed through the ship, and everyone knew that they were now ready to depart.

The vimana returned to the sky, rapidly gaining altitude as it followed the coast. It climbed higher and higher, reaching great heights for a long time, before abruptly changing course to the east. The now fully functional craft traveled at an astonishing speed, streaking through the sky like lightning. For three full days, the vimana continued its course, crossing vast oceans, towering mountains, and unfamiliar plains. The view from above was breathtaking: endless seas and seemingly untouched lands, with landscapes ranging from arid deserts to lush forests.

As the fourth day began, the ship slowed down. Now flying at a more leisurely pace, the vimana flew over the coastline before following a large river that cut through a lush green valley. The river seemed to be the path to the journey's final destination, for the vimana continued on its course until it reached a point where the river, as wide as a lake, spread out through a sparse forest. It was already dark when the captain decided to stop there for the night. Branco looked around, intrigued. This place was isolated, just the river and the surrounding forest; nothing else stood out. He wondered why the captain had chosen this particular spot.

At dawn, the soft glow of the sun illuminated the landscape, revealing a scene that Branco had never expected. The ship hovered a few meters above the ground, suspended in the air, and below it, a hundred ape men were waiting. Their expressions were serene, and their gazes turned respectfully to the vimana's commander. It was as if this moment had been long awaited by them.

The captain, with his imposing presence, called Harapa, Branco and the six dark-skinned men of the crew to descend with him. The group descended into the basket, which gently touched the ground, and as soon as their feet touched the ground, the locals formed an organized line. One by one, they approached the captain, greeting him with the traditional gesture of namaste, as if they were old acquaintances.

White watched everything with fascination. It was clear that the commander had a long history with these people, a connection he did not yet fully understand. After the last ape man had paid his respectful bow, the commander stepped forward. With a firm posture and a clear voice, he addressed everyone, speaking in a loud tone that echoed throughout the valley.

-- Friends, I have been around the world, I even brought some friends I met during the trip, but now we will have to go back to the mountains because I have seen many things and some very unpleasant ones.

I saw the action of evil on earth and it will grow in the minds of the beings of this world, it will dominate and distance them from the source that creates and maintains the worlds and peace will be extinguished so that they will no longer be able to know the way to return to the source and they will be lost in their own confusion, thus entering a forest of errors.

The Evil domination will manipulate the minds of the leaders and peace will flee from beings in such a way that everyone will become slaves of a destructive system and there will also be spiritual harassment that will not allow them to see the truth, making evil practically impossible to overcome. In the end, human beings will lose awareness of the truth and we will only be able to wait because everything passes, everything is impermanent, nothing in this world is eternal, only the creative source!

I will now leave part of my crew here and take one of them to the temple of the fish men and tomorrow we will set off for the mountains. The monkey man gave the usual greeting, together with his companions and the basket went up leaving on the beach the six dark-skinned men and the hunter.

Slowly the vimana began to rise and then head back towards the coast and then headed southwest along the coast of that place until the coast made a curve to the northeast and the vimana continued through the sea in a southeast direction and after a few minutes the large island that was the desired destination was seen.

Upon reaching the mainland, the ship slowed down and slowly headed towards the center of that place. They soon saw the site where the temple of the fish men was located, and the ship descended again until it was close to the land.

The commander called Branco and they both went down in the basket to find the King of the fish men, who was actually a man with dark brown skin like the other crew members, but besides apparently being as strong as the commander, he had a large dark beard and wore a coat that looked like fish leather covered in large scales, as well as a tall, pointed hat made of the same leather as the coat.

The King, who was already waiting near the place where the basket landed, came to talk to the commander who, after the necessary greeting, introduced Branco and explained that he needed lessons on astronomical navigation and that he would certainly be useful to that community.

There were several pools at the site, where they carried out various training sessions and they walked and walked around that incredible place, they went around some training sessions and returned to the vimana basket, the commander said goodbye and said to Branco – Soon you will have the opportunity to use everything you will learn here, use it wisely and always promote peace.

The commander climbed into the vimana, and the ship, with its usual enigmatic silence, disappeared into the sky, returning to the distant and mysterious point from which it had come. Branco, now alone beside the Fish King, looked around, trying to absorb every detail of that world that seemed to unfold before his eyes. The Fish King, noticing the young man's interest in everything around him, ordered his wisest subjects to instruct him in the ancient arts and advanced knowledge that his people mastered.

Day after day, Branco began to learn about the cardinal points and their importance for orientation, the changing phases of the Moon and how they influenced nature, the seasons and their cycles, and astronomical navigation, which was one of the greatest specialties of the fish men. The lessons were profound, requiring patience and concentration, but Branco was an attentive and determined student.

He was also introduced to the advanced machinery of the land. He was fascinated by the giant machines that worked with precision on the rocks, carving them and sculpting them into perfect shapes. He remembered seeing similar machines in other parts of the world, but those belonging to the fishmen seemed more advanced, capable of imprinting large pieces of solid rock with an almost magical ability. The stones were shaped into immense blocks, ranging from 1.5 to 2 meters long and 25 to 30 centimeters wide. Other smaller machines sliced these blocks, transforming them into thin slabs, used for paving or elegant parts of buildings. Branco watched this work with admiration, amazed by the precision and technical skill of the fishmen.

For months, his routine was disciplined. Every morning, he would accompany the Fish King on his activities and then spend the day immersed in learning. However, one day, a crisis struck the community. The largest of the machines, the one responsible for printing the grandiose stone pieces, broke down irreversibly.

When the engineers came to inform the King, the news caused concern. That machine was essential for the continuity of the works, and its loss would mean a major delay in the underwater civilization's projects.

It was at this moment that Branco remembered Harapa, the hunter. He had already demonstrated his skills by repairing the flying saucer, and the young man was convinced that Harapa could help restore the machine. When he suggested this to the King, hope shone in the sovereign's eyes. An expedition was immediately organized to search for the hunter.

The next day, Branco led the group on a journey aboard the fishmen's hovercrafts, machines that glided over land and water without ever touching the ground, as if powered by an invisible enchantment. They resembled modern hovercrafts but were larger and more sophisticated. They set off at dawn, moving with speed and precision. Two vehicles, each with three occupants, followed in formation and advanced toward the place where Harapa and the crew had been left.

The journey lasted four days, and during that time, Branco had the opportunity to reflect on his journey. He had not only adapted to the world of the fishmen, but had become part of it. When they reached their destination, they were disappointed to find only one of the old crew members, who explained that Harapa and the others had gone upriver, seeking to found a new community in the mountains.

Wasting no time, the group resumed their journey, sailing upriver for another day. The machines floated silently and elegantly over the water and continued through the vast mountainous landscape. It was only on the morning of the second day that they sighted the new community. Along the riverbank were several rudimentary buildings that indicated the beginning of a new settlement. There, on the riverbank, Harapa was waiting for them, although he did not yet know it.

When the machines stopped and Branco got out wearing the fishmen's hood, Harapa looked at him in astonishment, taking a few seconds to recognize him. At first, the figure dressed like the fishmen seemed strange to him, but as he approached, the old hunter smiled broadly in surprise. He had not expected to see his old adventure companion there, in that remote and inhospitable land.

With quick steps, Harapa ran towards Branco, and the two hugged each other tightly. "You came!" Harapa said, still in disbelief. "And what about the fishmen?" His eyes filled with curiosity, but also with happiness at meeting an old friend again. Soon, the formalities were left aside, and everyone sat down to share stories. The reunion was celebrated with enthusiasm, and Harapa, always willing to help, soon became interested in the group's visit.

--You know Harapa, I brought these people here because we came to ask for your help, we need to fix a machine and I remembered that you made that metal disk and fixed the vimana.

– What do you need to do to go there and fix our machine! Interrupted arrogantly one of the fish men who had piloted one of the machines and had approached the conversation stealthily.

Harapa slowly turned his face and looked at the man, startled by the sudden interruption. "I need to know what kind of problem occurred so I can know if I can solve it."

-- It has an image processing unit and it simply burned out, there is no defect, nothing broken in the mechanism, it is intact. The fish man replied.

-- There are no more parts to make this repair and we no longer have the means to remake the parts. I have seen these relics of the past being dismantled, and I think the best thing you can do is to put them at the bottom of the sea so that future generations will have knowledge of them.

The man dressed as a fish was furious and didn't say anything else. Regretting the trip, he got into the machine and sped off down the river, leaving Branco, the other vehicle and two of his friends behind.

After the angry man left, the others approached and Harapa invited them to see the place and the workshop he had built. Harapa had built a shed with brick sides and a geodesic roof, and in that shed he had finished assembling a machine with wooden and bamboo parts, a large loom that, as he said, would meet the needs of that community.

-- See this machine? It imitates the reality of matter to create another type of matter. It transforms this. He said, showing a roll of very thin rope. – Into this! And he showed a large piece of fabric that must have been about two meters wide and was rolled up on a piece of wood, making a roll that was almost one meter thick.

-- What do you mean, it imitates the reality of matter? Branco asked the hunter.

-- Yes, she builds the piece in layers, one horizontal layer and one vertical layer, in this way all matter has four senses within it, in the same way that wood, stones and metals are made, in fine layers, with tiny particles aligned laterally, one vertical and one horizontal alignment. Branco was amazed by his friend's ability but decided not to ask anything else.

After looking at how the loom worked, the visitors decided to leave. "Can you take this piece for me and give it to Josepho, the old crew member who stayed in the other village?" Harapa asked, referring to the piece of fabric. "Yes, we will do that right away!" one of the fish men replied. They left, placed the piece of fabric on top of the hovercraft and set off down the river.

-- Lynyrd, the one who went ahead of us, will ask the King to punish him for leading us on a fruitless journey.

-- And how could I know this result, at least I tried to help.

-- Yes, but Lynyrd is envious and likes to promote intrigues, in addition to having strong influence over the King.

The next morning, just before dawn, they arrived at the former crew member's house and were welcomed by him.

-- Did you find Harapa?

-- Yes, and he sent you a gift. Branco and the hovercraft pilot took out the roll of fabric to give to Josepho.

-- We think it's best for you to stay here in this community, ask Josepho for help until you settle in because it will be risky for you to return with us, because of Lynyrd. Said the pilot

Branco watched the old crewman, recognizing in his words a deep sense of need, but also a gesture of friendship. He understood that his journey thus far had been full of learning and adventure, but deep down in his heart, he had not found a place where he truly belonged. Josepho's offer sounded like an invitation to finally put down roots, to be part of something bigger than himself.

After a brief thought, his lips curved into a slight smile, and he gave his answer:

— Yes, I will stay here. — His words carried the certainty of someone who, after a long time, had found a purpose. — I am very grateful to the King for the teachings I received with his people. If you need me, I will be here or near this place.

The fishmen, always reserved, nodded to Branco as a sign of respect and immediately got into the hovercraft. The soft sound of the machine floating over the ground slowly faded away until it disappeared completely, leaving Branco and Josepho behind. The young man looked around and felt for the first time that this place could be his home. Josepho's simple house, surrounded by peaceful nature, exuded an air of warmth. He knew that his life there would be modest, but also rich in simplicity and meaning.

That same day, Josepho introduced Branco to his family, including his young daughter. When he saw her, Branco felt something awaken within him. Her green eyes, shining in the soft light of the evening, captivated him immediately. There was something in her posture, in the way she moved delicately, that fascinated him. It was not only her physical beauty, but also her attitude, her calm and dedicated way of taking care of the house and family. He felt an immediate connection, a mixture of admiration and curiosity for this young woman who seemed so at ease in the midst of that simple life.

As the days went by, Branco became familiar with the family routine. He took care of the animals, helped with the planting, and felt more and more part of that small community. One day, he noticed Josepho's daughter trying to draw on palm leaves, but without success. The lines were imprecise, and the material didn't seem to respond well to what she wanted to do. It was then that Branco, remembering Harapa's teachings, had an idea.

"I can help with that," he said, approaching gently.

The young woman looked at him curiously, and Branco began to explain. He remembered the technique that Harapa had taught him about creating writing surfaces. He gathered another type of plant from the region, and with a combination of layers, one arranged horizontally and the other vertically, he began to assemble a kind of rudimentary paper. The resulting material was much smoother and more suitable for drawing than the palm leaves she had been using.

"Try it now," he said, handing her the improvised paper.

She smiled gratefully and began to draw again, this time with much more ease. Branco watched in silence, delighted both by her skill and by the simple pleasure of helping her. The days passed, and Branco's presence in that house brought a new energy to the family. He became not only a helper, but an integral part of that little community.

On a clear, starry night, he and Josepho's daughter sat together outside the house, looking at the stars. The sky was particularly beautiful, with constellations that Branco could name and that seemed to tell him ancient stories. The young woman pointed to the stars, explaining what little she knew about them, and the two stayed like that for hours, in comfortable silence, sharing that moment of peace.

As the night wore on, Branco felt tiredness overcome him. The soft sound of her voice and the distant glow of the stars created an atmosphere of serenity that lulled him. His eyes closed, and before he knew it, he fell asleep there, under the starry sky, next to the young woman who was now part of his new life.

Then I woke up, I don't have the habit of opening my eyes immediately, first I try to feel how I am and wake up slowly, get up and everything else, I noticed that my body was a little sore, many hours sleeping I thought and noticed that some things bothered me, I tried to move my left hand and someone held me, I tried to move my right hand and the person stopped me too, I finally opened my eyes and saw a strange woman holding me, above her the ceiling fan was spinning slowly.

I thought about speaking, asking who she was, but there were tubes stuck in my mouth that prevented me from saying a single word and only by emitting a moan did I hear her respond:

-Don't move, calm down, it's okay! I'm Sabrina and I'm going to call your mother. That strange woman spoke to me in a soft voice and then immediately began to remove the tube from my mouth.

I noticed that I was connected to some machines, but I was in my room, I wasn't admitted to a hospital and I started to wonder what had happened. Did the woman say she was going to call my mother? Isn't she in Macaé? I looked at the bedroom window and realized that the day was starting to get light. What could have happened? How did I sleep for a few hours and wake up in this situation? I thought as the woman removed the IV that was connected to my arm.

Soon after, my mother came through the door and exclaimed, "Paulo!" And without saying a word, she came to my bed, leaned over, hugged me and began to cry.

- What did you do Paulo, I was so scared! She said emotionally, crying and hugging me.

I finally managed to speak and asked - Afraid of what? What happened?

I felt something bothering me in my penis, my mother moved away a little and I noticed that I was dressed in a hospital gown, in fact it was a catheter bladder that was bothering me.

Sabrina, on the other side of the bed, asked if I wanted the catheter removed . I said yes, and without any ceremony, she lifted my nightgown and slowly pulled out the catheter. Then she collected everything: the catheter, the urine bag, and the bandage she had applied to my arm. My mother watched everything without saying anything. She held my hand as if she were afraid I would run away, and I was beginning to understand my situation.

I had been intubated, they put a urinary catheter in me, saline solution, I even thought about asking how they did with other bodily activities but I didn't have the courage, after all physically I felt super well.

- You were hospitalized for twenty days, then thanks to your strange friend, we brought you home.

- Strange friend? Who was that? And why was I admitted to a hospital? I asked, already thinking about Mauricio, when my mother sat down on the bed next to me and began to tell the story.

- Marta found you unconscious in the living room, she thought you were in a coma because she couldn't wake you up and called an ambulance that took you to the hospital, then she called me, I came as quickly as I could and the doctors couldn't explain what was happening to you.

-After doing several tests and finally examining your brain, the doctors began to suspect that you might have been hit and become brain dead. But the tests showed that there was a lot of activity in some areas, which is not the case here, so a medical board wanted to operate on you, to do exploratory surgery and they came to ask me to authorize the operation, but your strange friend convinced me not to authorize it. He arrived just in time and said that you would probably die during the surgery and that if we didn't do anything, you would wake up fine in a few days. I was very afraid of the situation but for some reason I decided to trust that strange figure, now I think he saved your life. My mother said, showing her relief.

-And who was that, was it Maurício? Carlos?

- It wasn't a guy with long hair and a white beard, he said the name but it's a difficult name and now I can't remember it, I also don't know how he appeared there at the hospital

- A guy who looks like a hippie, with a leather bag and a baggy shirt? - Yes, that's the one! Dona Rosa replied.

-Shanerrai! – That's it!, that's right, he showed up minutes before the meeting with the doctors and told me not to authorize the operation, that you would certainly die if it was done, he told me details of the meeting I would have with them before it happened, then I went in and didn't authorize anything, the doctors then started to complain and my way out was to bring you back even though you were unconscious.

- Twenty days! How many days have I been unconscious?

- We don't know, Marta was the one who found you when she arrived from her trip and you were already unconscious, but that was almost a month ago.

- What did I do? Marta was going to be away for fifteen days, if it's already been almost a month, what day is it today? I asked my mother, amazed at what I had done.

-Today is July 3rd

- July 3rd, so I slept for almost two months!

-I think so, that's why it was necessary to put you on a drip and on this machine that introduces food directly into your stomach, now explain to me, why did you try to kill yourself, my son? My mother asked worriedly, perhaps thinking that I would try to kill myself again.

I didn't try any of that! Well, I had an unbearable headache, so I took a shot of some liquid I had saved and passed out, that was all.

-I'm going to call your father and Marta, she comes here every day, stays for a long time and didn't even go traveling because of you.

Sabrina and my mother left the fourth room for a while and I stayed in bed, thinking about all the trouble I had caused without meaning to and all the memories I had reached without believing that all of that had ever really happened, but, at the same time, they were memories coming from the depths of my mind in such a real way that even without believing it, I couldn't deny what were facts.

Minutes later, Sabrina brought me a tray with a very hot cream, a kind of soup that I don't know what it was, after that snack I heard the doorbell ring, I think my mother went to answer it.

Sabrina left with the tray and I got up to take off that ridiculous nightgown and put on my clothes. Soon after, my mother entered the room accompanied by Marta, who, when she saw me, hugged me.

– I want to beat you up, you crazy man! He said in my ear as he squeezed me and scratched my back.

- Why beat me? I asked cynically as if I couldn't even imagine the reason.

- Because you tried to kill yourself without talking to me, that's why!

- I didn't try anything, it was an accident! I answered quietly in her ear so my mother wouldn't hear, as I feared a barrage of questions about what had happened.

We sat on the bed and the doorbell rang again – My God, who could it be now? And my mother went out to see who was calling, returning a few minutes later with Master Shanerraiananda, dressed in his colorful shirt, white pants and carrying his leather bag.

- Finally, the imprudent one woke up! The wizard exclaimed as he entered the room, extending his hand to greet me.

- Good morning! I replied, a little scared by that unexpected presence. Minutes before, he would have found me lying down and dressed like a hospital patient. I greeted him and signaled for him to sit on a chair that was in my room next to the bed, and I sat on the bed next to my girlfriend.

- So, how are you? And the trip, was it good, was it useful? Asked the excited Shanerraianada.

- I'm fine but the trip wasn't very good, it was very calm but it was also very strange? I replied not wanting to show my discouragement.

- What do you mean strange?

- It's just that a lot of things happened that I have trouble believing, I saw things that I don't think existed in reality, but it wasn't an ordinary dream, so I have trouble accepting or not everything that went through my mind.

- What do you mean, I don't understand, can you give me an example?

- Of course! I saw myself in a gigantic building that reached above the clouds, it was a huge tower and it was a complete city, then a flying ship arrived and landed on a small balcony next door, then I entered a room that was part of the city building and there was a kind of hologram of the solar system with 12 planets, then there was a robot in the shape of a woman who told me about the destruction of some planets and that planet Earth was going to be destroyed too, but it barely escaped, only having its axis tilted.

-Continue! The wizard said with a startled look.

-Then I went out with another woman who was my companion and we went with a group of five other people flying in the egg-shaped ship, the people were all black with straight hair, there were no brown or white people, we went to a pyramid that was very far from the city, we went there to place some material on top of the pyramid and then we returned to the city building. But that was only the initial part of my trip.

-Shanerraiananda was watching me tell my story as if he was impressed with everything I said.

– Think about it, man only makes great works for transportation, food and mainly, energy generation, do you have any idea where this pyramid was? He asked me, somehow showing interest in what I said as if he knew something more.

I thought about where that pyramid could be. I had traveled in the flying egg and seen the Sun always on the rising side, most of the trip over forests and I remembered the giant tree that was on the way and a small stretch over the sea, but it was no use because I didn't know the starting point of that trip.

-- I remember passing a gigantic tree that reached the clouds.

-- There were many of these throughout the earth, their remains prove it, so it is not possible to know their location because of this.

-- I dare say that the pyramid was in Central America or on another planet because there is another detail, I remembered that there was no night, because there was a second Sun

-- It was the Scholz star that passed by here, but it did not pass through the Solar System alone. It was accompanied by an object known as a brown dwarf, a celestial body that does not have the mass necessary to generate fusion in its core but I believe it is a large emitter of radiation. When the brown dwarf passed by here, it destroyed the civilization that made the large blocks of stone, killing almost everyone, and the survivors restarted the civilization from scratch, which is why there is no record of them. Observations of the trajectory of the Scholz star suggest that 70 thousand years ago this invader passed within 0.8 light years of the Sun.

The wizard was once again thoughtful, as if he wanted to see the past – And what else happened there? Shanerraiananda asked, we heard the intercom ring, my mother went to answer it and then returned – Carlos came to see you, he's almost there. Minutes later...

-- Good evening! Carlos entered the room. My mother brought a chair for him to sit on, he put his backpack on the floor and sat down.

-- I went to the bank and they told me that you were hospitalized, so Marta called me today to talk about your recovery. Is everything okay with you?

-- Yes, I'm very well, it was, let's say... , an accident that put me out of circulation, but now I'm fine.

-- Did you fall off your motorcycle? Carlos asked me, a little surprised.

-- No, it was something else... I remained silent because I didn't know what to say because I remembered that Carlos was always warning me about the "danger" of regressions. After a few seconds, I looked at the magician and returned to the conversation. Carlos then realized that I didn't want to talk about the subject and remained silent.

-- As I was telling you, later I dreamed that I was in a cave and was a prisoner, but I managed to escape and went walking through a tropical forest when I saw a huge tiger that was going to attack me from the top of a rock, then a very bright and strong ray appeared that cut the rock in half and the tiger disappeared. But it was a long and very strange dream, full of fantastic creatures and super strange places.

-- What do you mean, fantastic creatures? Asked Carlos, who was a psychology professor.

-- Creatures like ape men, headless men, dog-headed men, centaurs and bull-legged men, as well as fish men, all appeared in my dream.

-- Well, these are not really fantastic creatures, they exist in some writings and in mythology. Fantastic creatures are those that exist in fantasy tales, as for headless men for example, there are writings from the past, including maps that speak of the Blemmys, monkey men, in India there are several legends that speak of them, the same thing with the dog-headed men, they were the cynocephali, there are ancient writings that portray tribes of them.

-- Do you mean it wasn't a dream? I asked a little scared because I was afraid of telling Carlos a truth that I didn't even believe in.

-- That's not it! Of course it was a dream. My friend said with a smile and continued. -- These beings no longer exist, but they are not fantastic creatures, they are legendary. They could be some archetype that your unconscious showed you for some reason. You saw them in books at some point in your life and stored them somewhere in your mind. Tell us the story from the beginning and maybe I can even help you understand it better.

-- As I was telling, the lightning was thrown by a man who was behind me and saw that the tiger was going to attack me, he was a tall and strong black man, with a full beard and a hunter-type jacket, and I became friends with him, then we left the forest in a kind of flying saucer and went to Atlantis, it was a circular and grand city with about 50 km in diameter, but I saw no movement there, there were only statues, all in sexual or sensual positions, looking like a representation of the Kama-sutra. The commander of the ship, who was the monkey man, asked if we wanted to get off there or continue the trip, my friend decided to go and I accompanied him.

-- Then we crossed the sea and arrived at a mountain where there were some giants. But the giants were machines piloted by some short guys, no taller than 1.5m. They had a formula that softened the rock that they scraped off and took to the other mountain, where they were building a kind of foundation and a large staircase next to it.

-- What do you mean they softened the rock, what rock?

-- They threw a liquid on the rock from the mountain and the rock turned into a soft mass, similar to concrete. Then the machines scraped that mass and took it in a kind of metal basket across the valley to another mountain where the construction was taking place.

Marta, who had been just watching until then, interrupted and said: How interesting, I've already seen that!

-- Did you see what my love?

-- A mountain where the rock appears to have been scraped off and there is a construction on another nearby mountain. Scholars say that the rock for the construction was removed from the mountain next door, but no one knows how it was done.

-- And where did you see such a thing? Carlos asked.

-- In Chile! When I went to visit the ruins of Ollantaytambo. My girlfriend replied.

-- That's right! I was here thinking about that place, I was looking at a photo the other day and there's a giant staircase that connects nothing to anything, it looks like they were terraces for cultivation, but cultivation at that altitude is very strange.

I was afraid I would blush with embarrassment at that moment and I squeezed her hand, wanting to say, keep quiet, no one wants to know about this, but I kept quiet and contained myself.

-- Continue Paulo, I'm sure it wasn't just that! Shanerraiananda pressed me, as if she was reading my thoughts.

-- So the monkey man decided to help the little big builder and traveled with the flying saucer to a place where there was a pyramid. He stopped the saucer on top of the pyramid and we got off, me, the commander and the hunter. As soon as we got off, the earth began to shake very strongly and for a long time. When the earthquake stopped, there were many people injured. Many inhabitants of the place had broken bones. The commander joined the chief of the place and they went to take care of the people. He had a kind of lantern that emitted a green light that healed everyone. They went to a very large hall and spent the whole day healing people with that light. The next day the commander walked to a large well, saluted the deity of the place, spoke to the people who were there, and we returned to the ship.

-- Did that pyramid in your dream have something on top, like a small cube, looking like a room?

-- Yes! I replied, seeing that Marta hadn't understood my grip on her hand.

-- And this well is natural, surrounded by rocks, isn't it?

-- Yes, why?

-- I was there in that place you mentioned when my father worked in Mexico, I took a tour there and went to El Cenote Sagrado, which is a well near the pyramid of Chicén Itzá. The Pyramid of the Sun.

-- You weren't in my dream! Carlos found my answer funny.

-- Then continue! Marta ordered.

-- Then the ship returned to the mountain of giants and there was nothing there anymore, neither the machines nor the short men, they had all gone. Then the commander decided to go further south over the mountains and we arrived at a large lake, after the lake there were some remains of their work and the group went down to see, we found another short man who was part of the group, who told the commander that everyone had gone down to the coast. The disk continued towards the west until it flew over the sea, then it followed the mountain range until it reached a passage to the other side, but the commander noticed that the land had risen.

-- What do you mean, up? Carlos asked.

-- I think the commander meant that the land had risen and not the sea level had lowered, something like, it had risen about 500 meters in altitude from what I could tell, he had previously said that an entire continent had sunk, then he spoke of these lands.

Carlos seemed thoughtful and moments later he picked up his backpack, stood up and extended his hand to say goodbye – Paulo, I have to go now, I'm late for an appointment, we'll talk more later and remember that I told you about the danger of those trips, take care! Then he greeted the wizard and left, Marta stood up to accompany him to the door.

-- So, continue with the story of your dream, we're enjoying listening! My girlfriend said as she entered the room.

-- Well, the ship then flew over the forest and arrived at a tribe with a river next to it and some circular buildings that had dome-shaped roofs. When I saw the people of the tribe, I saw that they had no heads, it was a tribe of headless men, in place of a neck they only had hair and they walked around naked.

-- And were there no women in the tribe or only men? My mother commented, making everyone laugh at my story and I had to wait for the laughter to stop before continuing.

-- There were three tribes with men and women, but they were all headless. In the first tribe, they hid and the ship passed straight through, only stopping at the third tribe and the group got off. One of the headless ones shot an arrow at the monkey man who caught the arrow in the air. Then he shot another at the hunter and missed, but he shot a ray back and hit one of them. Then the monkey man went there and with the magic lantern cured the being who had shot the arrow, but he didn't get up and the commander decided that we should leave.

--But if they didn't have a head, how could they shoot an arrow? Asked Sabrina, who was also paying attention to my story.

-- Well, they didn't have a head and their face was on their chest, their body was normal with their eyes near their shoulders and their mouth very close to their stomach. They just didn't communicate with us, they were silent the whole time and the commander decided to leave, saying that they were very ashamed for not being like other beings. Then the ship had a problem and landed on a beach, the whole crew got off and went to look for ways to fix the disk, one part of the crew went out into the pine forest and the other went hunting and built a clay oven for smelting.

So I took a break because I was tired. "Then you woke up?" asked Shanerraiananda, who until then had just been watching.

-- No, then came the strangest part. I spoke and then fell silent because I thought about going back to work at the bank. I should at least go there to find out how my job was going and get back to my life, but Marta interrupted me.

-- Go on, I won't say anything about the headless women, but I want to know who you were cheating on me with in this dream. My girlfriend said. - Or at least if there was an animal that would be a good guess for the animal game. Sabrina finished.

-- There were men with dog heads, like werewolves, men with bull legs and men who were fish men, but they weren't exactly fish, it was just the type of coat they wore and the strangest thing is that everything seemed very real to me but I don't want to believe it, it's too much fantasy for my mind.

-- Just so you understand, as your friend said, they are not fantastic creatures, these headless men existed, they were the blemmyes, the men with dog heads were the cynocephali and the men with bull legs were the satyrs, there is even the legend of the faun of the labyrinth, while the fish men are older and exist in the stories of the Sumerians. The wizard corrected me, a fact that made me continue the narrative of the "dream".

-- So the hunter went in search of minerals to make a part and fix the ship, after he returned he made some metal parts, some metal disks and fixed the generator of the disk that flew again and left, I think he went to the other side of the globe because it was a long journey, ending up in a valley that was his starting point, it was the region of the monkey men, then he went a little further in the journey, in the land of the fish men who were not fish, they were just clothes, from there I learned about the phases of the moon, the seasons of the year and about some stars, enough to know how to orient myself just by looking at the sky, then I returned to the starting point of the disk and ended up waking up here.

-- This story is kind of long, and you think it was just a dream? Shanerraiananda asked.

-- I found this story too fanciful to think of anything else, even if you believe that these creatures ever existed, it is very difficult to believe that they were something like memories from a distant past.

The wizard who was thoughtful for a moment – Maybe it was a warning from your conscience, just because you went too deep into your memories, she did it as a warning.

-- What do you mean, a warning from my conscience?

--That's right, you described the path of the serpent!

-- It wasn't a snake, there weren't even any snakes in the story.

-- That's not it, the path of the serpent is an initiatory path, it appears in writings about Kabbalah and also about kundalini, it is a path of ascension of energy towards consciousness. This path only occurs when the Chakras, in the case of Hindu study, or the Sefirot, in the case of Kabbalistic study, are not blocked, retaining the subtle energies. So I think that in your case, as you went very deep into your consciousness, this happened as a warning.

--But what kind of warning could it be, something like I should turn to some religion? Look for God in some way? Is that it?

-- It has nothing to do with religion, it has to do with your mental blocks that prevent you from being who you really are, from seeing the truth around you.

-- But what truth?

-- That you have many blocks in your life, that's all!

—Explain to me what you mean by that—I asked, still trying to comprehend the depth of the wizard's words. —Why don't I understand what blockage you're talking about?

Shanerraiananda, with his penetrating gaze, paused before answering, as if he were pondering the best way to explain what seemed to be a simple, yet complex truth.

—Look at the journey you described, he began calmly.

— First, you came out of a cave in a forest and a wild beast was about to attack you . This corresponds to the first chakra, the earth chakra, which is blocked by fear. Then, you were taken to the kingdom of Poseidon, Atlantis, which corresponds to the second chakra, related to pleasure, but there was no action, it was as if you were stagnant. Then, you went to a place where there were giants who were building and you had to leave there when there was an earthquake, this corresponds to the third chakra, that of strength, or the sephirot Hod and Nezah, reverberation and victory. And then, you met the headless men, who were dying of shame for being different, corresponding to the blockage of the fourth chakra, or the sephirot Tiferet, beauty, whose blockage is bitterness and sadness.

I remained silent, absorbing his words, as he continued, delving deeper into his explanation.

— Then came the cynocephali and the fauns, which correspond to the fifth chakra, or the sephirot Gevurah and Hesed, whose blockage is jealousy, lies, or lack of authenticity. Finally, the fish men and the monkey men that you mentioned correspond to the sixth chakra, the chakra of vision, whose blockage is illusion, or the sephirot Binah and Hokhmah, understanding and wisdom. Because of this, I believe that everything you saw was your own higher consciousness trying to send you a warning.

I was intrigued, still processing all the connections he was making.

—But what kind of warning? And about what, exactly?

The wizard paused, his voice now softer, but filled with wisdom.

— About your understanding. Understand! The journey of evolution of consciousness is something that most people do not even understand. In most cases, we are blind, or we only see in part, and our conception of truth is always incomplete. The Creator created an entire universe, with star systems and galaxies, which will always be inaccessible to the physical body. But in the subtle body, which resides in the universal consciousness, of which we are reflections, we will have access to the fullness of all creation. This, of course, as long as our consciousness is freed from the prison of the cycle of reincarnations, life after life, trapped in dense matter, in what we call annamaya kosha.

He looked me in the eyes, as if to make sure I really understood the depth of what he was saying.

— If you believe that you are made only of physical matter and that the proper functioning of your body depends solely on this, it is time to reconsider this concept. This thinking is as limited as believing that the voice you hear on the telephone can only be transmitted by wires. Whether we like it or not, we are forced to admit that the invisible exists.

He paused for a moment, and then continued.

— Wherever there is electricity, there is also electromagnetism. Although it is difficult to measure, we can see its effects. Our body generates electricity, a lot of electricity. Not only for muscle movement or brain function, but also for chemical reactions within organs such as the liver and lungs. A considerable part of this electricity is moved by the nervous system, which conducts this energy — bioelectricity.

Shanerraiananda seemed to become even more involved in the subject, his eyes shining as he spoke about the mysteries of the body and mind.

— The bioelectricity of our body can generate between 5,000 and 20,000 electrostatic volts. This would be enough to activate a Tesla coil, for example. In addition, the chemical reactions in our bodies generate heat, and all of this creates effects on the electromagnetic field around us. A simple example is electrocardiogram tests, which measure the electrical waves of the heart.

—So you're saying we emit vibrations, just like the Sun? — I asked, still trying to follow his reasoning.

"Yes, exactly," he replied. "We emit various forms of electro-magnetic vibrations, just like the Sun, although on a smaller scale, of course. Western medicine has only recently begun to explore these vibrations through tests such as MRI and radiation. However, our subtle body operates on a much deeper level."

He paused again, noting the impact of his words.

— We live primarily within the realm of the annamaya kosha, the most physical layer of our existence. Therefore, we experience emotions and reactions according to our gunas, the traits that bind us to the endless cycle of birth and death. And often, these cycles make no sense, as our energy is wasted on fleeting sensations, with no real gain.

I began to understand. The journey I had taken, the beings I had met, and the places I had visited were not just figments of my imagination, but symbols of something much deeper. They represented the blocks in my own consciousness, the obstacles I needed to overcome.

-- We are not these five koshas or sheaths, they belong to the lower existence and are strongly influenced by the Gunas, in the same way that we are not our lymphatic system, or the heart system.

-- The Kosha system refers to different aspects as layers of subjective experiences, these layers range from the physical body and are easily perceived, to more subtle levels of emotions, mind and spirit. Koshas are not individual "bodies", but rather systems, literally sheaths, in the same way that we have a lymphatic system, blood system, respiratory system easily identified by modern medicine, we have in the ancient writings of the Vedas the Koshas: 1 - Annamaya Kosha, 2 - Pranmaya Kosha, 3 - Manomaya Kosha, 4

- Vigyanmaya Kosha, 5 - Aanandamaya Kosha, 6 - Chitta Kosha and 7 Sat Kosha.

-- The ultimate goal of human life is to move away from the annamaya kosha and progressively strengthen the awareness and functioning of our being in anandamaya kosha, Chittamaya and Sat kosha, the universal consciousness itself.

-- Life without observing these objectives becomes useless for the evolution of the being, often resulting in unhappiness and frustration without the person being able to understand the real cause of dissatisfaction and dejection.

-- Denying our universal and divine nature, prioritizing instincts that are contrary to the evolution of our being, clinging to practices that are harmful to our physical and mental health is an act of extreme arrogance (PRIDE), for not recognizing our need for freedom that only has its correct expression and satisfaction in Anandamaya, free from illusions and deceptions.

-- Just like what Siddhartha Gautama , the Did Buddha do it? Martha asked while my jaw was still hanging open.

-- Yes, and for this He used a very simple type of meditation called Vipassana meditation, which prepares the mind for this objective. The defects that occur in a summarized way are:

The lack of **integrity** caused by the loss of love for truth. The lack of meaning in **pleasure** caused by the abuse of ephemeral sensations and the lack of understanding of reality, facts that can lead to the death of the spirit. The **ambition** to seek what is fleeting. **Loving** what is transitory and forgetting the purpose of existence. The lack of action (**laziness**). The **illusion** or belief in separation. The **arrogance** in making connections with the unreal.

-- So it has nothing to do with religions. My mother argued, who until then had only listened attentively.

-- What are religions? asked the strange Shanerraiananda.

-- They are the study of ancient scriptures that aim to connect man to God. Mrs. Rosa replied.

-- Ancient scriptures, you mean the Bible, right? Here comes Bomba, I thought as I heard Shanerraiananda ask.

-- Yes !

-- The Bible is a collection of books on astrology, magic and lost formulas. I'll just give you one example. In the book of Genesis, there's the story of Abraham. He's going to make a sacrifice to God. So he goes to the top of a mountain and takes two servants, his son and a donkey with him to a designated place. Think about it. What kind of God is this who needed a "sacrifice"? He needed him to go somewhere else and then asked Abraham to sacrifice his own son? Then He even made the lamb appear or "provided" for it? What's the point of that? What if the lamb wasn't really a lamb, but rather a reference to the era of Aries, which replaced the era of Taurus. After all, there were twelve tribes of Israel.

-- And what do the twelve tribes have to do with this?

-- It has to do with the zodiac. Have you ever stopped to think about how the stars can influence our lives? Most people don't even realize it, but our personalities and even our destinies can be connected to the cosmos. Ignoring these universal laws is like living on autopilot, letting astrological cycles guide us, without understanding that, in fact, we can use this to our advantage, to know ourselves better and align ourselves with the universe. Everything that happens in our lives, in some way, is affected by the stars, like the Moon, the stars... But only those who truly seek wisdom are able to interpret these signs and find a way.

-- And look how curious, in the past, humanity navigated the oceans using the stars, isn't it? Even the Bible seems to suggest that we should do the same with our lives, guiding ourselves by what is up there in the sky. However, in many places, astrology is seen as something evil, which is strange, because the scriptures themselves show that God created the stars, and they have nothing to do with evil forces.

-- Another great writing that was transformed into a great fallacy is the New Testament that was written by an Alchemist, but was used as a tool of control at the time of the Roman Empire, then they created the religion called Catholicism that dominated a large part of the world.

Then Marta, full of curiosity asked -- Written by an Alchemist, how can this be?

-- The knowledge that already existed before in the first humanity, that is, before the so-called flood, remained when the children of MU went to Egypt and thus remained among the wise men of that era. They had the ability to mold stones as if they were clay, transform other metals into gold and everything else that this knowledge provided them. Thus were made the pyramids and statues that to this day are impossible to replicate by common means. At the end of an entire era in which ancient Egypt appeared and reigned, the wise men handed over this knowledge, along with others, to the Roman invaders, but it had already been disseminated in other parts of the known world, which served as the foundation for some religions that would later be called pagan and also subjugated by the Romans. As an example, I cite the 12 labors of Hercules, an alchemical tale similar to the tale of the crucifixion of Jesus.

-- In possession of this wisdom, a Roman senator, with the aim of recording the knowledge that is expressed by a single formula, decided to write a novel with the intention of making it eternal for future generations. He wrote what we call today the "New Testament" and a few years later it would serve as the foundation for a new religion that initially united Roman soldiers and the people, and a few years later it dominated the world.

-- The holders of the formula acquired this knowledge and misused it, acquiring with it the power and wealth that accompanies this power and became corrupt, moving away from faith in the creator, they became corrupt by subjugating other beings to their whims and experiments and ancient science died in its principles.

-- Their goal was always to preserve alchemical knowledge, this knowledge was preserved throughout the ages, not by the adepts as there were always few, it was preserved in the stories they created, not to spread the knowledge, but to preserve it for generations.

-- So the whole story of Jesus and the twelve apostles is false?

-- No, an alchemist does not create falsehoods, but it is only a story! In fact, the twelve apostles are symbolic representations of the twelve signs of the Zodiac. Then came the change of the Taurus era, which was marked by the development of agriculture and the domestication of animals, such as cows for food. It is important to remember that this transition between eras is not about a fight between Christians and Jews, but about a symbolic change in our spiritual understanding. We are in the Age of Pisces, and the two fish that symbolize this sign are strongly linked to Christianity. A clear example of this is the biblical account of Jesus feeding a multitude with two fish and five loaves, a passage recorded in the Gospel of John, the two fish are the age of fish and the five loaves are the five senses.

-- Christianity, at its core, is strongly linked to the sign of Pisces. Many scholars have discussed the connection between the Zodiac and the figure of Jesus, although most people do not realize that Jesus is often a metaphor for the Sun.

-- And what do you say about other religions? My mother asked.

-- Most are tools of domination and control. Islam, for example, served to divide the Roman Empire. Do you know who said that Muhammad was a prophet of God? Himself! And he had political support to become known and popular. He founded a religion. In the same way, Buddhism. Buddha was a student of the Vedas, but they created another religion in his name, with offerings and worship. Understand one thing.

-- Take a deep breath! Said the wizard, then asked. -- Do you know what the most important thing in the world is?

-- Jesus, the conversion? My mother replied.

--What religion teaches you to be grateful for the air you breathe? asked the wizard, who was left without an answer, and continued.

-- The source that creates the worlds also created the elements and among them the air we breathe. Try going a day without breathing! We should thank the creative source for everything, including breathing, but no religion cares about this, they just want to indoctrinate and transform people into peaceful payers.

After Shanerraiananda finished that short speech, my mother stood up – I will prepare lunch for us and Shanerrai stood up too.

-- Paulo, I see that you are fine and I'm going to take the opportunity to go out. I took the opportunity and went to the shelf in the living room, took the little bottle with elixir and gave it to him.

-- Here is what is left of the elixir, I will not use it anymore, thank you very much, I will fulfill my part of the agreement as soon as possible. The wizard took the bottle, put it in his bag and we went together to the hallway to call the elevator.

-- I didn't quite understand what you said about the meditation that Buddha did. I asked Shanerraiananda before the elevator arrived.

-- It's like this: Buddha probably learned from ancient masters in India or Nepal a meditation technique called Vipassana. It's a very simple technique that you can quickly learn and develop. It enables the development of consciousness. Understand, people tend to think that studying and practicing spiritualism, clairvoyance, esotericism and everything else will bring you closer to God. But that's a mistake. We are part of God, a universal consciousness, or as I call it, the source that creates the worlds. So, only by developing your consciousness and improving your cognition can you achieve this understanding. The rest is fantasy created to keep humans away from this end. That's why you see so much perdition in the world. It's the actions of evil, it's that simple!

-- Okay, but how do I learn this, can you teach us?

-- For that, there is an intensive course that lasts ten days, just look for it and you will find it, we are in the information age! Shanerrai smiled, but I wanted to get a little more out of that master, something inside me told me not to let him go.

-- And as for my dream, I still have trouble accepting that *I "went back in time."*

-- In a way, time does not exist.

-- What do you mean, it doesn't exist?

-- Well, there are several things you have to consider, the first of which is that the number of people only started to grow a few years ago, in a much more dizzying progression from the middle of the last century onwards, which considerably reduces the possibilities of experiences for each of us. Another thing you should take into account is that time is much more our perception of the movement of things than the actual change of reality itself.

-- I don't understand what you mean by that?

-- I'll give you a more practical example. The wizard said this, and called the elevator

-Imagine that you have a dream, any dream, then you will tell me this dream, how long will it take to tell the story, even if you omit a lot of details.

-- I don't know, maybe ten minutes, I think it will depend on the dream.

-- Yes, but in reality the dream only lasted a few seconds, time is not exactly as you perceive it, the timelines, past, present and future, in a way happen at the same time. For example, where does the past happen?

-- It's happened somewhere before. I replied.

--But now it happens in your memory, right?

-- It's true, what exists are only memories.

-- Yes, and where are these memories?

-- In my mind, in my conscience.

-- And as for the future, it's the same thing, it exists only in your consciousness. What happens is that people's consciousness oscillates between past, present and future, never fixing their thoughts or their consciousness on any timeline, this is a subtle kind of dissonance.

-- So that world never existed? I asked the wizard.

-- Yes, it did exist, its marks are spread throughout the world and can be seen at any time.

-- This dissonance thing is quite interesting, can you give me your contact number so we can talk more about it?

-- I don't have a phone because where I live there is no signal, but you can contact me through Alberto, I go to his house every week. The wizard spoke and the elevator arrived

– What's really interesting is that you observe the things that disharmonize your mind, for example, the stereo sound with the music you listen to having a different sound in each ear, the films you watch, full of subliminal messages, the news that doesn't interest you, all of this only serves to disharmonize the parts of the brain.

I opened the elevator door for him – Ma'am! He said a namaste greeting to Marta.

Then he repeated the gesture to me – See you next time, Branco! He got into the elevator and went down.

My girlfriend looked at me a little suspiciously and asked – Why did he call you White?

-- He didn't do it, or did he?

-- Yes, I heard it clearly, he called you White!

Then I remembered what had happened in my last regression and ran to speak to the doorman on the building's intercom.

-- Hello Mr. José, a guy will come out of the elevator with a leather bag and a colorful shirt, please ask him to wait for me and I will go and talk to him.

-- Look Mr. Paulo, the elevator arrived here empty, no one has passed by here just now.

I was intrigued by the situation, but I realized that there was nothing I could do at that moment. The best thing to do was to try to stay calm and move on with my day. Marta and I went to lunch, and as the silence settled in between bites, I reflected on everything that had happened in the last few weeks. It seemed that life was leading me to profound changes, but I still didn't fully understand why.

After lunch, Marta sat with me in the living room, where a gentle breeze provided some relief from the heat of the day. She began to tell me about her trip to Dubai, but the expression on her face revealed that the experience had been more challenging than she had expected. In a calm but firm voice, she explained that although she had been paid well for the show she had participated in, the reality of the job was darker than it seemed.

"I received the most absurd proposals," she said, a hint of frustration evident in her voice. "The harassment was constant, and it wasn't just looks. People approached me, making offers as if I were just an object for sale. I felt so uncomfortable with all of this that, in the end, I decided to cancel my contract with the agency."

She sighed, and I realized that the trip had been a bitter experience for her, an unexpected lesson in the limits she was unwilling to cross. She continued, now with a more serene look:

— I've thought about it a lot, and I don't think I want to do this kind of work anymore. You know, Paulo, I prefer a quieter life, away from all this madness. In fact, I'm even considering moving to another city... starting from scratch, you know?

I listened carefully, understanding that she was going through a moment of transformation, just like me. Marta, always determined, now wanted peace, a simpler life. And, somehow, this touched me deeply. Her words resonated within me, as if they were the echo of my own concerns.

At the end of that afternoon, the Universe, with its peculiar way of guiding us, decided to show me clearly that changes were coming. As soon as I arrived at work, Sueli, my long-time colleague, called me for a private conversation.

— The bank's management has decided to dismiss you — were the words she said, bluntly, but with an expression of empathy on her face.

At that moment, a whirlwind of emotions hit me. The initial shock was quickly replaced by a strange sense of relief. It was as if a part of me had already known this would happen and was just waiting for the right moment. I didn't feel anger or despair; instead, there was an unexpected peace. I understood, in that moment, that the things that happen to us, even the most unexpected ones, are always for our good. As long as we are aligned with the goals of our conscience, the path reveals itself in mysterious but always precise ways.

A few days later, Marta and I were packing up our things to start a new phase in our lives. We had decided to move to a quiet town in the interior of the state, a place far from the chaos and pressure of urban life. The two motorcycles that had been part of our lives until then, symbols of freedom and adventure, were put up for sale. We felt it was time to trade that speed and movement for something deeper and more rooted.

We decided to buy a small farm where we could plant our own roots and start a simple but meaningful life. The idea of living surrounded by nature, far from the pressures and expectations of society, attracted us more and more. We dreamed of peaceful days, working the land, reaping the fruits of our own efforts, breathing the pure mountain air.

The change was not only physical, it was also spiritual. We felt like we were starting a new cycle, a new life, more connected to nature and to what really mattered. In that place, far from the distractions and artificial demands of the modern world, we could finally find the peace we had been searching for.

And so, with a light heart and eyes focused on the future, we left behind everything that tied us to a life of rushing and superficiality. We were ready to begin a new journey, together, in search of a simple, pleasurable and meaningful life.

www.ingramcontent.com/pod-product-compliance
Lightning Source LLC
LaVergne TN
LVHW010518200726
843506LV00013B/2638